The Crystal Messenger

PHAM THI HOAI was a young woman in her twenties when she wrote *The Crystal Messenger*. The furore that followed its publication caused her to leave Vietnam. She now lives in Berlin, where she previously completed a tertiary degree. She has since published a collection of short stories and a second novel, recently published in Vietnamese in the USA due to a ban on her work in Vietnam.

In 1993, the German translation of *The Crystal Messenger* was awarded the *LiBeraturpreis,* awarded each year at the Frankurt Book Fair for the best foreign novel published in Germany. Books by Amy Tan and Nadine Gordimer were shortlisted for the same award.

In 1994, she received a City of Berlin literary grant for her writing, which is now known across Europe and has been translated into seven languages.

THE
CRYSTAL MESSENGER

Pham Thi Hoai

Translated by
Ton-That Quynh-Du

HYLAND HOUSE

First published in Australia in 1997 by
Hyland House Publishing Pty Ltd
Hyland House
387–389 Clarendon Street
South Melbourne
Victoria 3205

National Library of Australia
Cataloguing-in-publication data:

Pham Thi Hoai.
   [Thien su. English]
   The crystal messenger.

   ISBN 1 875657 71 1.

   I. Title. II. Title: Thien su. English.

895.922334

Typset in Baskerville 11/12pt by Hyland House
Printed by Australian Print Group

Acknowledgements

I wish to thank Arts Victoria for the financial assistance towards the translation of this novel. I thank Mr Duong Tuon for making available for consultation his own translation of the first two chapters, Judith Rodriguez, Emma Burdekin and Priscella Allen for reading the initial draft.

I am indebted to Paddy O'Reilly for her valuable contributions to the final draft, Andrew Wilkins at Hyland House for his wonderful assistance and Dr Joan Grant of Monash Asia Institute for her patient support thoughout the project.

I wish to acknowledge a very special debt to the author for her views exchanged in our numerous and detailed discussions around the translation of this novel.

Finally I thank my family, Josephine, Cam Hoan and Cam Minh for their occasional but illuminating comments on matters of translation.

Ton-That Quynh-Du

CHAPTER 1
The Window

The house has only one room, sixteen square metres of brown glazed tiles; the room only one window, a rectangular opening sometimes blue, sometimes silky gold, most of the time oppressive grey, framing my glazed brown world. Four hundred brown square tiles and a magic ever-changing window, rotating like a Rubik cube.

The window doesn't open out onto any flowers. If it did I might have become a romantic girl but, as it is, I am violently allergic to any notion of romanticism. It's the window's fault. It doesn't open out onto any rooftops either – definitely not the kind of old tiled rooftops that I often see in the paintings of an artist my sister admires – otherwise I might have developed a sense of curiosity, keen to find out if what happens in strange rooms bears any relationship to the rooftop's muffled mumbling. I'm not curious; I don't have a rich imagination; I'm not romantic. My parents are quite right in feeling reassured about me.

The window looks out to a street leading up to a brewery whose rusty rickety gate squeaks twice a day. Twice a day my four hundred brown squares follow one another through the magic window, travel to the gate in a single file and return. That is the sum total of their lightning excursions.

Twice a day I study the human faces and forms. Once as they converge and vanish inside the gate, then as they come out of the gate and vanish again. I remain loyal to my own opinion of humans. There are only two types: those with a capacity for love and those without.

When I first began to study them, the crowd that poured out of the factory at knock-off time dazzled me. I used to have to pick out each individual carefully. Here was a girl with slender shoulders, delicate to the point of dissolving in the infinite patience reflected in her eyes. I gave quiet advice to the men of this world to rush to receive the unlimited tenderness that she could give. Here was a man, middle-aged, dependably muscular, with jet-black hair and a warm smile. I pictured a small mushroom-soft hand in his large strong hand and felt a gut-easing sense of peace. And here was a young man, flat forehead, with thin, determined lips. He was strong. I feared that strength. If he kissed a girl she would be crushed like an insect.

There are faces that look as if they have never smiled at anyone.

Over fifteen years, many people have passed through my classification process. Their identity, their occupation, age, blood type, appearance, whether they are gross or slender, good citizens or outlaws, virginal or have tasted all the murky temptations of life, feet firmly planted on the ground or floating somewhere ... none of this is important to me. What is significant to me is whether or not they are capable of love. That is my only criterion for placing them to my left, near my heart, or to my right. My position at the window is the position of a judge. One can study, classify and control the human race from an ever-changing rectangle such as this. All that one needs is an unwavering belief in one's own intuition. I disregard the never-ending debates between my sister and her numerous lovers about right and wrong, about relative and absolute, about the finite and infinite-ness of other systems of reference. They will continue to argue all their lives about matters unconnected to my philosophy, which is predicated on love and gentleness.

Nowadays no crowd can make me feel confused. Months and years spent by the window, my only task to classify humans into Homosapiens-A, those with a capacity for love, and Homosapiens-Z, those without it, have given me a sharp and sensitive n-th sense, sharp and sensitive to the extent that only one second is needed to screen a whole mixed crowd. Of course, many oscillate between A and Z. Sometimes I have to wait a moment before lifting them up to their place on my left or my right. But this is the only task that is meaningful to me. I have worked diligently and responsibly, patient as an unromantic, incurious, unimaginative accountant, for fifteen long years, regardless of whether the colour outside my window is blue, silky gold or oppressive grey.

Yesterday afternoon he appeared. Close to the window. The deep and permanent wish in me is to be able to caress a man closely hugged to my chest, breathing in the smell of the other sex. If I had just put my hand through the window I would have been able to touch him. But instead, I contracted myself to a minimal volume and obliterated all means of communication: limbs retracted, chest compressed, hair ingrown into my head and brain, and breathing kept to the minimum.

For so many years I had practised this inward contraction exercise. This time it was a brilliant success. He was smoking a crumpled cigarette, his eyes cast towards the factory gate and he didn't see me, a small snail clinging to the ledge of the window.

My rectangle suddenly turned into a dark yellow parallelogram. End-of-shift siren. The thick jet-black hair left my arm's reach. Apart from the crumpled cigarette he was also holding a bicycle pump. I had imagined a violin.

This afternoon he is bound to come again. My capacity to wait is unmatched.

CHAPTER 2
The Rain

Why is it that during July and August the rain is so plentiful and rainwater so briny? It must be that the four oceans of the globe gather together to thrash down on the incessantly leaking roof of my house. If not, there must be someone weeping on the roof. How else can rainwater be briny?

I grew up without once tasting mother's kisses. Briny rain. Bland soup. Even blander lessons at school with half-awake students and semi-comatose teachers. Some bitter memories. And lovely sweet midnight dreams, although occasionally interrupted because mother and father did not have a separate bedroom, and mother was convinced that the children wouldn't hear a thing.

I am the youngest child in the family. In fairy tales, the youngest child always grows up before her time, in order to gather in all that her parents and older siblings cannot understand.

Each time the roof cried, mother would grit her teeth:

'Everyone else manages to find oiled paper to fix their roofs, how come you can't? Theirs don't leak, how come ours does? Why can't you see the leg of this chair needs fixing? Why on earth did I have to marry your kind, my God!'

I, the youngest child, the voluntary silent stenographer of the family history, even before learning to read and write, had started to collate these 'why' questions into double helixes resonant with the sounds of rain. They twisted around my neck like an uncut umbilical cord, throttling my pubescent dreams, dreams about a harmonious loving couple: a wife who never asks questions beginning with 'why' and a husband who never smashes up the furniture. I can't live like father and mother. A hundred times no, a thousand times no.

Life was smothered by the leaking roof and rickety chairs, and there was no room for kisses. Kisses were luxuries that my family could not afford.

Father would also grit his teeth:

'Other people are different! I have my honour to guard! I have my pride! Here's for the bloody chairs – crrrash, here's for oiled paper – crrrash!'

And finally, sobbing cries.

So our family quarrels continued, along the theme of honourable pride. Honour and pride smothered our family, stronger than any bunker's roof. We took shelter under their shield as if it could render us invisible to the world. The world consisted of neighbours, colleagues, relatives and friends. Friends we did not have, a luxury we could not afford. Harsh, unforgiving pride forbade father to 'organise' some oiled paper to patch the teary roof. Honour could not be violated, it had to be preserved even at the cost of love. Honourable pride was what justified the existence of our family.

I have grown up thirsty for love. For me honour and pride are far too abstract. Even if the whole human race worshipped me – and why not? – my heart would be too weak to respond to five billion heartbeats, my lips too small to hold five billion kisses. I only long for the tenderness that I am capable of picturing in my poor imagination. I only long for a gentleness that I can absorb and am capable of returning. These would prove that my existence is not altogether without meaning. Pride and honour are too abstract and do not promise anything.

Homosapiens-A and Homosapiens-Z: my window divides humankind into two. I walk on the sea of humans and they divide themselves into A waves and Z waves. Homosapiens-A long for love but their longings are rarely met. They glide past each other like asteroids of the mysterious cosmos, occasionally colliding by chance and leaving wounds that never heal, dormant-volcano scars. Their union is so rare; it only happens once every two or three centuries. My body carries a volcanic fever. I am frightened of collisions that bring injuries. I name those wounds sadness. Deep sadness.

When I was ten, the war forced us to evacuate to the countryside. I attended Year Five at the village school. At the end of each class, the teacher, Kien, would always be on all fours looking for his thongs which had disappeared into a corner of the classroom somewhere. Every day, invariably, one of his thongs would escape and travel right round the classroom under the tables. When he spoke in class, his mouth frothed like the falls of Da Lat. He once taught us, 'You don't know it yet, but butter is a type of meat that is sold in cans.'

One day it rained and a few drops of rain fell right on my desk. I cried uncontrollably. The class was dismissed and teacher Kien took me home and personally handed me to my parents, saying, 'Perhaps little Hoai is not quite right in the head.'

My fifty-one classmates began to ostracise me.

CHAPTER 3
Little Hon

In fact, I am not the youngest child of the family. Fate dictated that I replace little Hon in this position.

She was not any age; I cannot imagine her as having an age, I cannot imagine anything about her. She came and went. Like a messenger from above visiting this world on her never-ending journey.

Little Hon came into this world when my mother thought that she could no longer have another child. One day our washing was left outside overnight. Strangely, only my mother's underwear became wet with the evening dew and showed patches of dark stains. Mother hesitated. She always hesitated, torn by indecision. Then she shrugged, 'Lucky nobody pinched them. Oh well, it's only underwear, not something people can see.'

Such was the attitude of my parents towards matters that were out of sight. But my sister Hang was obsessed with her underwear, she chose it as she would her soul-mates. I wonder, if it wasn't for the important year of 1975 and the noisy invasion of the consumer world – corsets, TV, whisky, underwear, all very sophisticated – flooding in from the southern half of our country, what would my sister have chosen to be the soul-mates of her body's nether regions?

Not long after that, my mother fell pregnant. My parents were in two minds: four children were already more than enough, a worrying burden at meal times. But father said stoically, 'God gives and God provides.' And mother chimed in, 'Yes, a gift from above, why not accept it? We've got nothing to lose.' It may well have been the only time that my mother ever chimed in harmony with father.

As she was born, the little girl did not cry. Instead, she smiled at the thirteen nurses standing around the bed. In response all thirteen of them, after the initial surprise, began a chorus of cries, with my mother, in extreme panic, leading the choir. They stopped crying when my father came in, and the little girl again smiled at father, a smile that threw him backwards into a chair. It was not the smile of an infant. Little Hon was never an infant. Her smile was one buried deep in time, a message from her unending journey, which sometimes surfaced gently for the world to see.

She ate little, slept little; she mostly smiled. She never revealed the secret of her age to anybody. She had beautiful flowing hair and the velvet eyes of a young girl. The cheeks of a three-year-old. A mouth that gave enigmatic but friendly smiles to all around her. Lovely translucent skin, white and pale. A fragile and gentle crystal messenger. Mother said that in this world, no other child was so easy to look after.

She would lie in her tiny cot, quietly asleep, and awaken to generously dispense her soul-capturing smiles to all around her. Her smiles caused us to tiptoe, to talk in gentle tones and to regard each other in a kind and enlightened manner. Those were wonderful days. Our dull, ordinary family routines suddenly became simple and sacred rituals. The weeper on the roof stopped singing his bitter and briny songs. The rickety chairs ceased to squeak. It was as if a magic wand had been waved in rhythm with a rare, smooth pulse of life. Those humans whose vocal chords had seemed to know only how to emit aggressive grunting noises, whose faces had seemed forever engraved with life's harsh worry lines, were suddenly transformed back to their original innocence. The world turned bright, clear and mild, like the face of a child asleep in a cot. Happiness came so suddenly and was so breath-takingly simple.

Even my oldest brother Hac, the most difficult and disrespectful in the family, mellowed to the point of weakness. Every morning, the first one to wake up, he would tiptoe to stand guard near the cot, waiting for the first smile that little Hon would give to the new day. Then gently he would open the door, fetch the water and wash our mountain of clothes, and only then would he wake everyone up. Around this time, just deserted from the army, he was driving a *cyclo* around Hanoi and did not hold high hopes of life. Mother was surprised. 'What has come over him?' Father was sceptical and dismissive. 'It won't last ten days.' My brother only smiled, a true Homosapiens-A.

But soon came the warning signs. Sometimes when father came home, tired and unhappy from endless problems at work, either to do with his colleagues or with the lousy pay, he would sink into a chair, pick up his pipe and raise it to his mouth but would stop, and put out the match at the last moment to swear at the smiling little Hon, 'Wipe that smile off your face. What are you smiling at? Nobody is smiling with you!'

The wheels of human psychology are complex. They need just enough oil to function smoothly; too much of it can make the cogs too loose and ruin everything. Father's machine is monotonous, and it seems, the more monotonous the more difficult to understand. How was little Hon to know this? She could not put a stop to her crystal smile, no more than the cicadas could their singing. As it turned out, all the tiptoeing, the care, the gentleness were luxuries that our family could not afford.

Not to mention the kisses.

When she learned to speak, little Hon was able to say just the one phrase: 'Give me kiss.' On her wobbly little feet she moved around the house with her arms, slender as two blades of *lau* grass, open ready to embrace anybody, her little rosy pink lips jutting out in the perpetual request 'Give me kiss', and, in her generous way, giving out innumerable baby kisses perfumed with a milky fragrance. My family reeled under her unceasing cascade of kisses. Our faces were always wet. She did not care what we were doing, what pre-occupation we might have; her need for a kiss commanded the world to stop and respond, even if bombs were falling overhead.

But humanity had more pressing needs than kisses. Mother would often get irritated, 'Go somewhere else. Enough! I am too busy!'; and father would grumble, 'Stop, stop! Enough! You are making my face all wet!' Not so easily discouraged, little Hon would continue tottering around the house looking for someone else more receptive. When nobody was around, she would sweetly ask the tabby cat 'Give me kiss', and the cat never refused.

I also never said no to her. I was prepared to accept all the undistributed portion of her love. But the little girl, like all generous people, possessed a profound sense of equity, and persevered, going around her world of four hundred brown squares to reach all those who had not yet received their fair share of kisses in life.

If only those who had not received their share would freely call out for help.

If only all those who looked as if they had never been able to smile could be enlightened by the crystal halo emanating from this precious little girl.

On the day my oldest brother received notification to re-enlist, little Hon came sidling up to him and asked, 'Give me kiss'. At first he paid her no attention, looking piercingly at a fixed point on the ceiling, playing with his fingernails. After a while he gruffed, 'Piss off!' and brushed her aside. She fell down, her friendly smile unchanged. Odd that it was he who used to stand guard next to her cot, waiting to receive the first magical smile of her day. Another machine gone to rust.

The next day little Hon did not wake up. The whole family was busy seeing my brother off and nobody as much as looked at her. Holding the tabby cat, I bent down over her tiny cot. Her eyes were closed and a friendly smile was on her face. Afterwards mother would say, 'I had mistakenly thought that she was asleep.' Mother always 'mistakenly thought'.

But little Hon never woke up again, the fragile crystal messenger who had entered this world by mistake, giving out kisses and smiles. She did not need anybody to close her eyes for her. She was adequate in herself, and for everything around her. She went, taking with her the mystery of her strange presence in my family. Why my family? Father said, 'A gift from heaven returned to earth.' My parents had nothing to lose when she came. When she left, they also had nothing to lose.

It was a cold and bitter winter's day. To the last minute, her lips remained bright like two little glowing embers lost in an otherwise grey and cold world. When they came to take her away, I hid under the bed. So did the cat. I did not cry, on account of her smiles. The messenger of love came, showed her patience, and left, a bird fleeing snow. I could only hope for a warm day that would bring her back.

Mother lost her capacity to speak for a week. When she regained her voice, she could only utter bitter recriminations. Several days after the funeral, the cat also left. Three years later, my oldest brother Hac was discharged from his border post in time for the exhuming of her body. When they opened the coffin, it was empty, clean, tidy and fragrant; the only thing remaining was the ever-friendly crystal smile of an expelled messenger. They cremated that purified coffin and also burned her smile. This completed the obligations of those who remained.

Fate dictated that I became the youngest child of my family. I was not a gift from above, and the earth below would not take me.

CHAPTER 4
Sundays

The essence of my feelings about Sundays: wet.

From Monday to Saturday the six weekdays race ahead without stopping to have a drink, so Sunday is meant to be wet. From five in the morning, all things that can safely come into contact with water line up in a queue for the public water tap: blankets and sleeping mats, pots and pans, chopsticks and bowls, clogs and thongs, hair and flesh, four hundred brown squares, dozens of thoughts suppressed for six cracking-dry days. The great weekly baptismal rite goes on until all – things and humans – shine in their peculiar Sunday cleanliness. The rite continues till five in the afternoon, sometimes longer, because my family is but one among hundreds of fanatical believers waiting in a line in their pilgrimage to the only public water tap.

The terrible jostling scenes at that sacred place left in me a terrifying impression about the fellow members of my species. They brawl and abuse one another, they expose the darker secrets of each others' lives, in their fight to become clean. They prepare their cleansing rite by splashing all the suppressed filth festering inside themselves on the heads of others. Public catabolism of a verbal kind. The rite has become a fashion, its faithful adherents turned into just a sea of Z waves capable of swallowing and drowning everything else. People who in their normal daily life are so patient and kind, friendly to the point of being forward, trusting to the point of being naive, change beyond recognition once they reach this sacred Sunday place. Angry, aggressive, non-compromising and belligerent. Sudden mutation. The fault of their double helix? This is why my rejection of the fanatical Sunday crowd is a purely biological reaction.

In the evening, when the last pilgrims have happily returned to their homes satisfied, when the newly cleansed consciences are drifting into sleep resting on newly cleansed pillows placed on newly cleansed mats, drifting into newly cleansed dreams, I, the small snail, would crawl to the water tap. Two forgotten beings. I would remain silent and the tap would wastefully sing an unending hymn, without key, without crescendo, a steady nocturnal lullaby.

Several times they have tried to turn off the tap but without success. I am happy; please continue to flow for no-one, please do not dry out, do sing forever this nocturnal lullaby, do not turn silent like me. It would be sad if we were both mute.

It was on the day of *moc duc* – the feast of purification – that little Hoai suffered a five-hour baptism in order never to become a woman.

I was fourteen, 125 centimetres, thirty kilograms, pigtails. For the first time I saw my own blood in its most puzzling form. It was not like a wound, nothing hurt inside, nothing hurt outside, not sensational as with my sister Hang's case. A week earlier, she had cut class and run home, triumphant like a weight-lifter who had just broken a world record. 'I have become a grown woman!' What a huge weight! I only felt disgust, the same disgust I felt towards other waste substances expelled from my body. To me the signs of becoming a grown woman were just as meaningless as weight-lifting records. Didn't my sister understand the price she would have to pay for that one-day victory?

I quietly went into the public baths, filled up the shallow bucket, sixty centimetres in diameter, sat snugly inside it the way I used to as a child, and a sense of peace rose in the opaque windowless darkness. The plastic bucket, which had grown smaller with each birthday, suddenly returned to its original form, a vast lake in my three-year-old's trouble-free memory. I tucked my chin between my knees, happy in this foetal position, safe in mother's womb, and drifted into a sleep resonant with the fountain's lullaby. Foetal sleep: I did not want to become an adult.

I avoided touching my emaciated body. For fifteen long years since then it and I have had many occasions to look at each other. But this time I ignored it. I forgot everything. I did not even hear the sound of pounding on the door. Father broke down the door to the bathroom and carried me, half-asleep, away from the bucket full of dark red water, a sunset-coloured lake, in front of the dozens of pairs of eyes, frozen in anger and fright, of those pilgrims waiting for their turn. They had been waiting for five hours. Buckets and tubs, washers and soap, dirty wastes that needed to be discarded, all piled up, a huge nine-headed dragon at the door to the communal bath house.

My five-hour rinse finished off my period once and forever, every ounce and every drop, erasing forever all capacity to become a woman like any other woman, an adult like any other adult in this world. A record to surpass every other record in this nation.

Now I am still fourteen years of age, 125 centimetres, thirty kilograms, with pigtails. At first mother and father were worried; my four hundred brown squares constantly sweated the smell of herbal medicine of all kinds. I could not avoid the absurd confrontations with men and women in grimy white coats, their face the same sickly *congee* colour as their attire. I couldn't tell them the secrets about a vast dark red sunset lake enveloping my eternal foetal sleep, could I? It would be of no use. Afterwards my mother sighed and clicked her tongue in a gesture of resignation. Like accepting a bad karma. Or an eccentric habit.

My sister Hang is twenty-nine, older than me by less than a minute. Each time she steps out from the public bath house, she looks like a mermaid.

CHAPTER 5
The Book Collection

Nowadays nobody mentions that book any more, the book that marked a turning point of my life, *Early Season Longans.*

It was a day when my whole family was out, and by default I became the owner of the world of four hundred brown squares. I locked the door, held the key tightly in my hands and began to enjoy the role of mistress of the house. I do not remember how I attacked father's huge collection of books, the tempting forbidden garden. Before that day, my knowledge was confined to lessons about butter being canned meat *à la* teacher Kien; to copies of *Progressive*

Youth magazine, bicolour, cheap and kitsch; to a few *Golden Youth* stories written by condescending adults. Father guarded his book collection like a dictatorial God guarding the forbidden garden.

Dazzled by a forest of new and wonderful things, I closed my eyes and selected a book, not too thick, not too thin, *Early Season Longans.* It was a war story, guns and deaths. The only thing that I remembered was the love story between a beautiful woman guerrilla fighter and a muscular soldier. No, what mattered was not the love story. Love stories dominate fairy tales, don't they? They do not amount to anything more than simple moral fables, often simplistic to the point of being stupid. Old fairy tales evoke in me the sickening feeling of having to listen over and over to what is already well-known. But in reality, what did I know? This cheap novel made my mouth water. I fell into a state that I had never known before. The whole lower half of my body ceased to function normally, teetered in weightlessness, then fell into an indescribable crevasse. A white body hesitantly appeared under the vast moonlight, her light brown guerrilla uniform torn to pieces, the strong thirsty hands of the clumsy man reaching for her quivering full breasts.

In the middle of a locked room, I removed all my clothes and cried in self pity in front of the lost fourteen-year-old girl in the mirror. My hands searched my stunted breasts determinedly, but without feeling, without the magical trembling sensation. This third-rate book brought my innocent childhood to a conclusion.

Afterwards, many outstanding books reached me, but none of them ever managed to erase the decisive impressions left by *Early Season Longans*. There are lucky people whose doors to knowledge are ornate, orthodox and official, opening onto a shaft of light shining on proper icons. They only need to travel that well-lit path, stand beneath those icons, and they know for certain that somewhere, another door, also ornate, awaits them. My door reeked of dirty sweaty flesh; behind it was mysterious darkness, sinful but irresistible. I do not envy those other doors. I am forever grateful for that most important event in my life, regardless of its questionable worthiness.

In the evening, when my family gathered together, I listened to the inconsequential chat and smiled in tolerance. If only they knew! But it was to take me a long time before I fully understood the meaning of the considerate noises coming from my parents' bed at midnight.

That night I dreamt of a moonlit beach, a guerrilla uniform left at the foot of the waves. I shivered and woke up. My whole lower half felt numb with incredible pleasure. Next to me, Hang was deep in sleep. I undid her buttons and admired her in silence. Even now I still have not grown out of watching other women's breasts, craving to caress their white skin and flesh. My sister Hang: 'Are you sick or something?'

Luckily for me, my father was an obsessive collector driven by two major motives. First was to be able to display his collection as a declaration of a rich and healthy intellectual life, one that rarely had an opportunity to surface in a life full of daily teary rains and rickety chairs. Second was to be able, in his retirement, to open a shop renting out books. The picture of an old man, silver-haired and bespectacled, standing by shelves of books was probably the final dream in my poor father's life, a life not blessed with many dreams. The richness of his intellectual life and the likelihood of realising this dream varied in direct proportion to the number of books acquired. They were always 'extremely rare, very hard to get, had to go through insiders' types of books. Without exception, father would inscribe clearly the date and place of purchase – 'Second-hand book shop on Ba Trieu Street, late autumn'; 'The Combined Literature Book Shop, an afternoon in mid-July' – and put his own complicated signature on the first page, and then on page seventeen of the main section, affirming his inalienable right of ownership over this part of humanity's cultural heritage. Poor father.

After *Early Season Longans* I fervently attacked other doors. Three-quarters of what I found were third-rate, a starvation diet whipped up for non-discerning stomachs.

The Gadfly did not move me. I refused to join the game of hide-and-seek, half-hinted mysteries, wound-up thrills, man-meets-woman plots contrived for the sole purpose of elucidating some very relative qualities such as bravery and cowardice, honour and dishonour. It was simply a badly written old story, a little too long for an old story. A work that had everything, except honesty.

How Steel Was Forged was even more disingen-
uous. Perhaps not the writer's fault. He probably
believed his own tales of heroism and convinced
many others to believe them as well. The title of
the book and its main character, Pavel
Kortshagin, aroused in me the wish to keep a
distance, away from things that are too strong,
too rational, too inclined towards heroic achieve-
ments. His pronouncement on how life should
be lived '*in order to, on the point of death, feel that I
have not wasted my life*' drew a meaningless line
between life and the other world, posed an
absurd question, a very forced question about
the meaning of life. Yes, the meaning of life, even
I pondered incessantly about it within the
narrow confines of the four hundred brown
squares and a magic, ever-changing window.
How could he pose a question that fudges the
essence of life like that? He clearly didn't know
about the crystal messengers who come and
leave, giving without asking why, mysterious
and delicate, like my little Hon.

Those two books shaped the intellectual face
of a generation. With a choice between the
gadfly or Pavel Kortshagin, they walked, talked,
loved and thought within a pre-made uniform
labelled Voynich or Ostrovsky. Apart from these
two books there were a few other accoutrements
to add a sense of variety – richness and liveliness
within limits – such as *Jane Eyre* (wet melodrama
with a good ending), *Baron Von Goering* (drench-
ing melodrama with not such a good ending) or
Pautovsky's *The Yellow Rose* (sweet melodrama
trying to be non-melodramatic, as usual).

I refused to join that generation. I refused to have anything to do with those strange characters; I rejected any mass-produced uniform.

Other generations were more fortunate – or more unfortunate, who knows? – being born into other intellectual uniforms. My parents probably grew up with Scholochov and Balzac, with *Saturday Romances* and the *Self-reliance Writers*. Baudelaire, Lermontov, Chekhov, all French or Russian. If forced to make a choice, I would wish the next generations a cultural journey stronger in substance. Don't ignore any part of the globe, and most importantly, don't forget the land under your feet.

I refused to join any generation. I refused to wear any uniform too tight or too loose. Let me be with my own naked, scrawny, stunted body.

Yet one book managed to accompany me throughout all these years: the lonely Don Quixote. At first I dismissed him; he was lost amidst my unending quest for stories of love, real and unreal. Until, startled, I began to follow his hopeless but poetic struggles against more than just the well-known windmills. I cannot say any more about him, any more than I can say about my recurrent dreams, dreams about things that cannot happen in life.

From then on, the world of books opened the most unexpected doors for me. I meandered in this labyrinth, without a thread to guide my path. Often I would reach a destination only after travelling a tortuous path and even then, looking back at the mountains of books behind was not allowed.

Driven like a person possessed, I established new records for book consumption. I swallowed many without properly digesting them – a habit of those starved for a long time – and they piled up inside undigested. It took a long time before I, the child of a poor family, learnt to master the proper way to enjoy sumptuous banquets of humanity's cultural heritage.

Each of us had our own style. Father enjoyed books by ensuring that the great thoughts from East to West coexisted happily, if clashing noisily, next to one another in his bookcase, by firmly sealing them behind hard covers – paper coffins for a mass funeral, serious and elegant. Mother was not concerned with culture – an instinctive reaction, a survival reflex – and this did arouse in me a small sense almost of respect.

My oldest brother Hac shared her attitude, but with him it was a conditioned reflex. The alarm bell that regularly rang during the huge 31-year experiment that was his life had wiped out forever any sense of affection he may have had towards anything smelling of culture, or 'reeking of culture', in his words. He left school at the age of thirteen, smirked at father's family pride and honour, shrugged his shoulders at mother's pleading eyes, worked as an ice-cream seller, ticket scalper, *cyclo* driver, joined the army then deserted, rejoined and re-deserted, and finally de-enlisted to become an operator of an illegal gambling racket, a business that involved only the series of natural numbers from zero to ninety-nine. He said numbers had fuck-all to do with culture.

My second eldest brother Hung was the important bridge between the first, wasted son and me, the most burdensome and youngest child. His completely neutral attitude towards the world of books was indicative of his whole approach to life. He was calm and moderate, knew a little bit of everything, was a touch passionate about everything, comprehensive but superficial, intelligent enough to be happy about himself, sufficiently kind to avoid causing others harm; a necessary conjunction linking many complicated and lengthy sub-clauses to the main clause, curt and short. A part of the wiser younger generation, he avoided father's footsteps. Sealing books in paper coffins wasn't for him. He approached books in the same way he would football and beautiful girls. My family and relatives admired him without reserve.

When it came to the twins Hang and Hoai, books were like the air we breathed. After graduating from university, Hang went to work at the National Library, the biggest library in the north. I ceased to have to rely on my father's extensive but non-discerning collection. My sister became my most loyal source of books, even though she would hand me the books with the condescending air of an easy-going ticket inspector turning a blind eye to children entering a cinema to see an adult film. Birds eating the same fruits but popping out different droppings. We were sisters breathing the same air yet she became an outstanding woman – intelligent, sensitive, ambitious – and I could never cross the threshold to the adult world, despite the fact that I had set foot in father's forbidden garden and absorbed the sins of my forebears.

With many other families, the reverse happened: huge collections of books handed down from previous generations became dispersed by neglect. The luckier bits ended up in second-hand book shops, the remainder at paper recyclers, or worse, at the bottom of pots and pans or in public toilets. But then again, education and knowledge have nothing to do with the essence of Homosapiens-A.

This afternoon, he again came to my window, with his hand pump and his crumpled cigarette. I am sure he has finished Year Ten, but in this day and age, what would a high-school certificate mean? He doesn't strike me as a keen reader, at least he seems not to have the time to read, even casually. But he is A from head to toe. One in a million. Fate has pushed him within my reach; there are those who are born to belong to each other and I have been waiting for him for so many long years beside this window. But having shown so much patience, at the decisive moment I panic, fearful that making a move now might spoil the whole thing.

CHAPTER 6
Brownian Motion

How much love bloomed in my time at school, the childhood of a girl who was always the smallest, the oldest, and the best student in the class?

The objects of affection were of course the teachers, great men in the eyes of the students, especially the teachers who often looked at me in class. Our teachers needed, and sought, the *yes, I understand* look in the eyes of the best students; otherwise how could they have enough confidence to go on teaching what was largely baseless nonsense? But I interpreted pedagogic eye-contacts as signals of romance. How could I have done otherwise? I had been waiting for too long. Every eye that searched mine contained a look of love, without discrimination, without reserve, without perspective. Whenever I moved up a grade, I would forget the old teacher and become submerged in the eyes of the new teacher, just like the Brownian Motion of physics, chaotic, random, uncertain. Over time my childhood school days blurred into a thick mass which I have now neither remembered nor forgotten. That undead past is not active either, it lies dormant somewhere like an inactive volcano. And that is most dangerous.

For ten years my sister Hang and I sat at the same table, shared the same books, the same tests and examinations, and also the same looks cast our way.

The older she grew, the more beautiful Hang became. After her weight-lifting record, achieved at the age of fourteen, her clothes had to be continually unpicked and resewn larger. A fire danced in her eyes, on her hair, on her flesh, a fire that stunned everybody around her. Every night I would undo the buttons of her blouse and follow the impatient progress of her breasts as they became those of a young woman, full and firm. Occasionally, opening our shared books, I would find crumpled letters with the handwriting of pubescent boys, clumsy and insecure. Surely it was not for those insipid boys that my sister changed – physically and emotionally? 'Just rubbish. Young bees itching to try out their bees' dicks.' Where did she learn such bold language? In Year Ten Hang became the beauty queen of the whole school. She grew before her time and learnt sadness early in life.

One day, the teacher on whom I had a crush stepped onto the teaching platform but his eyes did not stay cast in my direction as usual. Instead his gaze glided indifferently past me, stopped elsewhere in the general direction of the class, and left me waiting.

I sat there quivering, my whole body tense, my eyes fixed on him. I followed each gesture of his hands and watched the way he stood, the expressions on his face, a face so familiar to me. The class dragged on like an execution parade. Not once did he look in the direction of the window where I was sitting, slowly becoming fossilised. His voice no longer had its usual energetic warmth, full of care and trust, which I had thought especially reserved for me. As the school's drum sounded the end of session, he hurried out before the class had time to stand up to bid him farewell. He did not even give a nod of acknowledgment, leaving the students looking at one another in bewilderment. Precisely at that moment I understood: next to me was a vacant seat; my sister Hang was sick, she was absent.

How come I had never realised this before? How could I not have known for whom the teacher's attentive eyes were reserved? Desperate longings had turned into illusions. The advantage of being born one minute earlier was indeed cruel. She had blossomed out of her twin sister's stunted growth. I had received all that was repulsive and ugly for her to accept, in her innocent way, all that was attractive and beautiful. The

Creator, in the post-inspiration moments after creating such a wonderful creature as her, picked up the odds and ends and created me while He was at it. But what of the fairy tales about twin sisters who were exactly the same? What about Thuy Van and Thuy Kieu? The Creator was not at fault. The fault was mine.

I cried again as I had done five years before, on a rainy day when raindrops fell on my desk. This time nobody took my hand to lead me home, even if only to complain about my not-quite-right state of mind. I cut class and went for an aimless walk along the city streets, returning home at midnight with the expression of one who has just given up suicidal thoughts.

The following day Hang returned to class, sat next to me, and the piercing glances of the teacher once again swarmed towards us, thick and fast, focusing at the place where we sat, burning her feverish cheeks. But I had already become an iceberg, inert and cold. I did not want to enjoy vicariously the warmth reserved for somebody else. The Brownian Motion ceased at that point. Around me everything became quiet, motionless and without soul.

Several months later we completed school and Hang sat for the foreign language college entrance examination to study French, encouraged by the young teacher with a strong passion for Victor Hugo. Father and mother, after many arguments, for the first time agreed with one another on the serious state of my health: the circulation system, the digestive system, the respiratory system, and especially the nervous system of little Hoai did not allow my parents, very responsible parents, to encourage me to continue to climb the educational and social ladder. My inner icy mass would not melt. The time for random diffraction had finished and a huge vacuum opened up, swallowing up my world of four hundred brown squares and an ever-changing window. I said to my parents: 'Yes, the Brownian Motion has finished. I want to stay home.' Those were my last words before I became an autodidact, due to education denied; an outsider, due to not setting foot outside. Father and mother exchanged worried looks. I didn't quite add that I refused to climb any kind of ladder, especially those leading to tertiary education and the pyramid of social status.

I don't know what the other people of my generation went through.

From Year Five, the complex of being ostracised never left me. I avoided the curious mocking eyes of my friends. I grew more and more withdrawn, performed better and better in all subjects, and became more and more desperate for some empathy. I finished high school with the maximum possible marks, ten out of ten in all four subjects. In order not to cry again in front of strangers, for the next five years I hung on to the ledge of my window.

CHAPTER 7
The Disaster

In the summer of 1975, before entering university, Hang was a most beautiful girl. I admired her unreservedly and I was happy to accidentally receive admiring looks cast her way, with disastrous consequences for many years. Her temperament had changed; she had become moody and impulsive, her movements unpredictable. On account of the nine months that we had shared in the confines of our mother's womb, she was frank and open with me, treating me with the confidence one would feel with children, reassured by their innocence.

Sometimes I acted as her messenger, delivering

magnolia-fragranced letters to our Year Ten literature teacher and receiving from him perfunctory
pats on the head. The Brownian Motion fever
had just finished. I was tired but alert, and I could-
n't see anything in common between myself and
a placid man just over thirty, already married
with four children. He had deep-set eyes lost in a
smooth face with a roundish chin. I saw quiet
pride in his quiescence, kindness in his face, intel-
ligence and determination in his eyes. Perhaps I
wasn't wrong. It's quite possible that he had been
or could have been like that. Everyone is either a
has-been-something or a will-be-something, like a
parabola – full of promise but unable to rise
above its own limit.

I laughed as I pictured teacher Hoang as a
parabola limited to what he had (wife and four
children, the modest salary of a level three
teacher, Victor Hugo) but striving towards what
he wanted to have (Hang, coffee and cigarettes
every morning, Victor Hugo). He stood to lose
nothing by investing Victor Hugo into this
venture of passion. He had had a small collection of poems published in the respected
Literature and Art magazine under the pen name
Hoang Van – 'Prince of Literature' – and several
hundred others not yet published. V.H. junior
was still patiently polishing his prose. But then
again, he taught literature and wrote poetry.
Mathematical symbols were not his strong point.

One day Hang asked me to go to the movies
with her to the *Ruslan and Ljudmila* epic – a
movie suitable for children. I did not like
rehashed old stories, but Hang needed me – who

doesn't need someone else of smaller stature? As the lights dimmed, I felt hot breath at the back of my neck, uncontrolled heat emission. On the screen was a simplistic film, a black-and-white moral lesson, but my sister wasn't watching this two-part third-rate movie. Teacher Hoang was sitting behind us. His hands and breath, both above normal body temperature, pulled her into a quiet but determined struggle from which I absorbed the total radiated heat, wastefully beamed in the direction of my icy core.

Hang: 'I don't want that. It will not lead us anywhere.' Oh, her seventeen-year-old language!

Hoang: 'Don't think like that, darling. In the final analysis, where does life lead us anyhow?' Oh, his profound thoughts!

Hang: 'No! Life must lead us where we want it to lead!' She squeezed hard, not his hand but mine.

Ljudmila: 'Ouch!'

Hoang: 'You are still so young. Life still holds so much promise, so you think like that. I am now past the half-way mark of my life and I know there isn't much to hope for. I have only you ...' His ambitions contracted suddenly.

Hang: 'No I can't ... I've got to go far, far away.' Oh, Jane Eyre!

Hoang: 'Don't be so cruel. I need you. Don't turn your back on a drowning man.' Ljudmila was floating on a flying carpet. She was asleep.

Hoang continued: 'One day you'll remember what I've just said. You'll understand.' The heat source behind me increased by several hundred watts.

Many years later, thinking again about that ridiculous declaration of love taking place among the scenes of love and killing set in the Middle Ages of Russia, I felt compassion for Hang. She truly grew up too soon, enveloped by sadness before her time. Hoang needed her and she needed me, the dark side of the moon, sometimes full, sometimes not. If we could only articulate it in a language like that of mathematics: if a needs b and b needs c, then a needs c.

Disaster took place on an early autumn evening, the only time she went out without me, her little but loyal protector. When she left the house she even winked at me. I stood there for a long time, transfixed, thinking about the way she walked, a white rose without thorns. With my parents, I was able to advance thousands of perfect reasons to protect her, covering for her even within the family. That evening was heavy and interminably long, like an impending storm refusing to shed its rain. As I have said before, I am not curious, not blessed with a rich imagination, not romantic, how could I have sat by the window and accompanied my twin sister on her journey to a certain promised land? I could only feel anxious. By intuition I grew increasingly aware of an impending disaster. I wished it were a twin disaster so that I could share half of it. She and I shared so many things, our food, our books and our New Year money; we even shared the chores of sweeping the floor and washing up the dishes ... everything was shared equally. But from the time when she continued to grow and I stayed stunted, she had started to grant me privileges, accepting less for herself, regarding me as her younger sister, not a sister one minute behind her but a generation. Everyone, and most of all my sister, began to forget my true age, and sometimes even that I existed. The power of invisibility didn't just exist in old stories.

I stayed at my window until very late. When she came home her gait was different from when she left. Stealthily I negotiated around all the obstacles on the floor: first my parents' bed, then Hung's one-metre-seventy length and the one-metre-seventy-five length of Hac, all strewn across the sixteen metres square, to come close to the quivering white rose.

'How can I take a shower now?' That was all that she said, her only comment on the event that turned a girl into a woman. My power to become invisible proved useful. In a minute I brought everything she needed for her midnight rinsing. She had showered before she went. Between the two showers, the eye of the storm. I stood in front of the public bath house, mentally prepared to stand guard for five hours or for the whole night. Half an hour later she came out. The rose had been crushed. Five minutes later we were lying next to one another, she still stunned, I hurt and upset. She cried in silence, turned and held me in the same way one would hold a little doll, and hid her tears in my hair. 'I'm afraid ... I'm afraid,' she said. Silently I undid the buttons of her blouse, caressed her breasts as a child would its mother's, allowing her to drift into a heavy sleep punctuated by the sobbed refrain 'I'm afraid ... I'm afraid.'

Even my hair felt feverish. I lay awake all
night waiting for that man Hoang to show his
face from her dream so I could slap him really
hard. But the drowning man did not emerge.
Fate allowed him to surface once more in her
unfortunate life, much later, by which time she
had consigned this experience to the tangled
morass that she regarded as the past. This experience did not simply rob her of her virginity, it
also buried forever all her desires of the flesh.
What was it in her Homosapiens-A qualities that
prevented her from turning her back on that
man? Why on earth didn't she simply refuse?
Would she ever enjoy the pleasures of giving, of
surrendering herself in love? Would life lead
where she hoped it would? Where would this
door, its hinges forced open, lead her?

In the following days her worry increased to
the point of alarm. Mother started to become
suspicious, despite my faultless eloquent explanations. The 'honour of a cadre's family',
already injured by the wayward son Hac, now
assumed the defensive spiky pose of a cornered
porcupine. One day, in extreme desperation,
Hang ordered 'Come with me' and dragged me
to a place beyond human imagination.

It was a little attic room filled with twilight
dimness, thick with cheap but strong incense,
reeking with undefinable smells. The occupant,
male or female I wasn't sure, sat quite still somewhere in the room and occasionally blessed the
surroundings with a couple of grunts in a
hoarse, severe voice. We placed our money, five
piastres, the sum total of our New Year money

collected the previous year, on one of the numerous dirty plates on the floor among the grimy incense holders, in exchange for a packet with mysterious smells wrapped in dirty old newspaper, and took leave apprehensively.

I threw up when we left that place. Hang vomited when she closed her eyes and swallowed the slimy contents of the packet that cost us all our New Year money.

The dim attic room and that packet were permanently etched in my memories of life's dark, powerful forces. Teacher Hoang had nothing to do with those forces. His function was that of a drowning man. He had a lot to do with thinking reeds; a junior Victor Hugo living out a real-life *Les Miserables.*

I never knew the true impact of those dark forces. I only knew that Hang's body began to function normally. The signs of disaster were erased. She became quiet, stayed home a lot and never went out with anyone. I ceased having to yawn at the cinema during those boring didactic films amidst absurd declarations of love. At the end of October, she went to university, taking with her the heavy baggage of an autumn of birth and death. She never mentioned it to anybody. No-one else in the family knew. Years later, among friends discussing the growing sexualisation of love among the young, she would simply laugh. It was then that I noticed the contrast between her laughter and my smile. Even my smile stayed stunted, in order that her laughter could burst through and soar high on a celebratory note.

The dark forces of the past didn't forgive her easily. She was unable to conceive again. I know that for a child she would be prepared to exchange anything and everything, from her exquisite beauty and her husband with a fetish for toilet paper to her dozens of lovers.

But the debt of sin owing to that packet remains. She is lonely.

CHAPTER 8
The Faces

He had no age, no occupation, no family. In this city there were many like him whose identity was not revealed in any sociological statistics. Nobody wasted their time asking about him and he did not waste his time asking about anybody, or about anything – rational or otherwise – that occurred around him. Even those around him felt no need to know what he did, how he lived and loved or how he amused himself, let alone the government. Members of his species were distributed all over the place, from wharves, stations, markets, to streetside tea stalls, places where humans were as nameless as the air, like the froth that formed and dissolved, formed and dissolved, caught in the unfeeling wheels of the sugarcane crushers.

Sometimes, finding himself in a strange location, a park where tall trees and rows of lights stood in a permanent salute to the silent paving stones, an inaccessible villa where armed soldiers stood guard against sparrows, an imposing department store with revolving doors engorging and disgorging foreigners – babes in the woods and brazen little brats – he would whistle, not in a disapproving way, nor quite admiringly, then quickly return to his lair, his dominion covering over three-quarters of the city.

The first time I saw him under my window I went numb. He did not have a face. Unlike millions of other people, instead of the inseparable face, above his neck was just a blank, without boundaries to define it from its surrounds, dissolved, dispersed, completely wiped out by a remorseless invisible wiping rag, a suspended vacuum just hanging there.

The faces that presented themselves under my window generally sorted themselves out. Oval, square, round, oblong, tiger faces or mouse faces, thick or thin, worried or unworried, angular or smooth, full of life or devoid of life.

There were ample faces, overfilled, glasses of frothing beer, beaches full of people which refused entry to late-comers. Ample faces without any tissue that could be further bloated. Faces of those only eighteen or twenty years of age yet already so satisfied, pleased with themselves. There were faces that pretended to be ample,

satisfied and secure for no reason. Faces bulging
to their limits – hydrogen-filled balloons wary of
sudden wind-gusts blowing the wrong way.

And there were hungry faces, with deep eye
sockets like bottomless craters swallowing the
disasters of their lifetimes, the black holes of the
world absorbing everything, the way an empty
house absorbs the wind. Tired and weathered
faces, engraved with the ravages of life, empty
and hungry with unfulfilled desires, waiting like
the final resting place. Fathomless faces, or open
doors ready to entice any passers-by.

For many long years I had trained myself in
order to be able, within a second or so, to pick
out those hungry faces amongst the mixed
crowd. In the end, everything falls somewhere
between A and Z. There were those who carried
with them a stack of faces, truthful and false,
noisily clashing with one another. And those
who wore a series of faces showing one at a time
– the principle of modern television – each day
presenting a different one to the idle public. And
there were those who always wore a mask,
immovable masks like limpets on ship hulls.
And those who did not even have a complete
face, only two-thirds or even just a half of a face,
something missing, destroyed, and the remainder long dead, lifeless like benign tumours that
no-one had the heart to remove.

But he had no face. His faceless species was
everywhere, the incognito tribe occupying
more than three-quarters of an incognito city.
Surely he would have been born with a face. It
was still there: ear, nose and mouth, teeth and

hair, lips and eyes, but only soulless geometrical shapes remained; the rest had long been deadened by the cruel grind of life. Life's eraser performed its purging function not just once, but day by day, peeling back each layer of skin, levelling each deep crease, taking away all those elements that constitute the face of an individual human, so that by the time he appeared under my window he had been reduced to just a shape, distinguishable from others only by weight and height. It was difficult to recognise him among his kind, copies from the same mould lucky to escape the fierce competition between strong personality types. He merged into the crowds, into the street dust, into contemporary novels and stage plays; dissolved easily in those solvents only to crystallise and reappear as himself, the person without a face, the person who has lost his face, the person who has forgotten his own face, representative of the pitiful and terrible incognito tribe.

From time to time he came into my field of vision, whistling in a way that was neither friendly nor pretentious. Without fail, I would freeze in terror and impotence.

Then he started to appear in my dreams, at first as small as my little finger, then growing and multiplying into many figures of the same shape, masses and masses of his type, mountains of his species, growing and growing, blocking my breathing passage. A whole division of the incognito army, with him in the lead, collectively raised a threatening finger and announced: 'Dismiss!' and my face slowly

fell down into a huge vacuum. Dissolved.
Dismissed.

Nightmares without a human face.

CHAPTER 9
Model I

At one minute to zero hour of 29 March 1979 Quang the dwarf appeared under my window: 126 centimetres of biological length framed in a blue pullover, yellow trousers ironed into two stiff columns, and a new pair of sand-shoes, their whiteness accentuating the red of his socks. Thus dressed, he stared at me, one hand holding a bunch of red roses, the other a postcard, also of red roses.

At precisely zero hour of her twentieth birthday, little Hoai received her first declaration of love. On the same day, three years before, he had declared: 'When you turn twenty I will tell you something important.' He is the only person who remembers my real age. And who keeps his word, the most true-to-his-word man I have met in my twenty-nine years, a miniaturised man whose word can always be trusted. He remembered my birthday while I had forgotten the meaningless numbers existing in the dozens of papers that legitimise our life. Unfeeling signposts to reality.

Very early in his life, Quang the dwarf realised the need to remove these signposts, and, in their place, to erect new ones, marked out in black and white, unmistakable goals for a solitary marathon. But alas, there is but one glittering prize for so many jostling competitors. Who will win the crowning glory? Who will taste the sweet juice of the grapes? I had thought that he, an undersized grain too small to survive the screening process, had given up in self-pity. But the dwarf star had not left the sky of hope and desire. Three years, then two years, and then again three years, it kept reappearing according to its fixed orbit, never forgetting its promise 'I shall return', never veering from its course marked out by those black-and-white posts.

The first goal in his life, a life unblessed by nature, was set when he gathered sufficient scientific evidence to determine the reason for his stunted growth: hormone deficiency. No more illusion, it's not malnutrition, nor a temporary halt in growth. At fifteen years of age, seventeen, twenty, and now at thirty-one, he is still just a little taller than a ten-year-old, his body developed in proportion. All its parts – public and non-public – are there, a genuine pygmy king. Even his face hasn't aged, a face forever round, clean, mocking time. Only his eyes reflect the suppressed desires burning within and the will to conquer the terrible fate that has denied him a drop of hormone, causing him to live his whole life with the miserable word 'dwarf' attached to his name.

Now and then he would come to my house for a visit, his hair parted in a perfect straight line, on his chest his sparkling Communist Group insignia, in his hands a black notebook with a bright gold pen enclipped, and above all, with his twin status as both an old school friend of Hac and as the Secretary of the local Group. He would always knock, clear his throat, wait for an appropriate time, politely step in, greet everybody, then take serious steps – steps far too long for his body – to his usual place at the table, sit down, cross his legs and remain silent. Father usually held him up as a good example to Hac. He would pour Quang tea as he would someone of his own stature, because every time there was a local meeting, Quang would always be either its Secretary or would chair its voting panel. My parents perhaps didn't particularly enjoy these visits by Quang the dwarf; they didn't quite know how to address him. But they tried to show him respect in such an exaggerated way that they themselves grew to half-believe their own serious words. My brothers summed him up with the well-known character prediction, 'Worst, crossed-eyes; second, dwarfs.'

Only Hang talked to him, at first just being

sociable, and later, finding him 'interesting and amusing'. Yes, Hang needed many of these 'interesting and amusing' things to blunt the sadness that came so early in her life. Quang the dwarf would sit there in silence, his back straight, his coconut-head perfectly still. Occasionally his burning eyes, fiery like two glowing charcoals, would glance away from the portrait of the revolutionary Che Guevara that mother had brought home to cover the termite-eaten parts of the cabinet door, briefly immerse in Hang's two glistening eyes – I could hear the sizzling sound of the fiery coals meeting Hang's moist eyes – then in a daze return to Che.

At the age of twenty-one, 125 centimetres from head to heel, he wore his red armband and stood guard during the successful post-unification monetary reform. The first confrontation with that despicable monster, money, forged in him an uncompromising attitude to any manifesta-tion, however refined, of decadent capitalism, rotten pragmatism, and cowardly individualism. Nearly ten years later, he was again entrusted with the mission of confronting money, and again, Quang the dwarf engaged in his task with enthusiasm as he would with any future mone-tary reform that took place during his lifetime. No, he had nothing to do with my Don Quixote. When he dies, and is placed he won't be thinking about the huge meaninglessness of fighting against those windmills. When he dies, and is placed in a coffin too large for him, he will smile with satisfaction, 'I haven't wasted my life.' A Pavel Kortshagin, a miniaturised copy, certified.

To celebrate the success of the first monetary reform, Quang formally invited Hang out to have ice-cream at the Thuy Ta lakeside pavilion. The beautiful third-year French student opened her eyes wide – 'Ice-cream?' – but she accepted. Seven o'clock that night, after the familiar knock and clearing of the throat, he appeared, red armband still pinned to his white poplin shirt. Hang took my hand and tipped her head in a 'follow me' gesture to her six classmates, some bespectacled, some wearing loud shirts, well-dressed city playboys and brave heroes forever in search of an excuse to heap praise on the beautiful Manon Lescaut. A dark shadow crossed Quang's face, but the oversized self-confidence packed inside the undersized pocket of flesh did not desert him in this awkward situation. In a serious tone he invited 'all the friends here to have an ice-cream on this great day of the nation'. Then, holding his head high, he led the group, his red armband the beacon guiding them all: Snow White, one dwarf, six giants, and the little snail.

The lakeside was beautiful at night. For twenty-four hours a day my window took in the yeasty brewery smell but now I was confronted with the smell of the lake. I became all lungs, breathing deeply to take in this oasis of nature hidden in a city of a million people, its eyes always open to witness everything around it: festival fireworks, trams leisurely picking up commuters laden with daily necessities, the unceasing stream of state office workers on bicycles, the ever increasing army of Hang Dao Street traders threatening an invasion, time-calls emitted by loudspeakers and answered by the large square clock of the post office, the furtive but passionate caresses of lovers who dare not hold hands or kiss in public yet have nowhere else to go.

I wondered if the eyes of the lake had witnessed Hang's disaster at sixteen?

I did not participate in the fun and games of Snow White, her one dwarf and six giants. The giants talked in a language 50 per cent their mother tongue, 20 per cent third-year French, and 30 per cent their own language, a student code not shared by outsiders. I'm an outsider. Quang is an outsider. The tertiary education system, predicated on the four pillars of Intellect, Morality, Strength and Aesthetics, rejected him – the dwarf star – from their sky dotted with faded, ageing supernovas. Intellectually, he's better than millions of others. Morally, a born cadre like him cannot be lacking. Aesthetically, under a magnifying glass he is no different from others. The problem is physical, a question of strength, the fault of the missing drop of hormone. Universities rejected him: with your health, how can you cope with the increasing demands of the revolution? He accepted their rejection in silence, his eyes burning more and more with suppressed fire.

After several futile attempts to initiate the hot topic of the success of the monetary reform, Quang shrank back into his seat, his legs dangling hopelessly, not quite touching the ground. It seemed that Hang and her six classmates simply forgot about him. They ate their ice-creams and talked to one another in their proud mixed-code language, laughing and singing. Quang the dwarf lit a cigarette, crossed his tiny legs, and blew out smoke in a serious fashion. His face was in the shadow. Occasionally his burning eyes and the fiery tip of the lit cigarette flared in the dark, three phosphorous corners of a surreal triangle. Surreal, that is, until a strong, firm hand slapped him on the shoulder, removed the cigarette from his mouth and threw it into the lake. 'Who said you can smoke, child?'

Startled, the students turned and watched, some curious, some visibly enjoying the unfolding spectacle. He got up slowly, stretching all his 125 centimetres from head to heel and looked up at his antagonist, a strong well-built young man wearing an identical red armband. The young red guard waved an index finger: 'Too young to smoke, you understand?' Then his finger, about to press on Quang's forehead in admonition, changed direction and pointed to the red armband pinned to the pygmy prince's arm. He said to himself, 'Oops, what's this?' and whistled in surprise.

The monetary reform and the red armband saved Quang the dwarf from an awkward situation. He accepted the apologies proffered by his colleague, waved his hand in the dismissive gesture of a superior, rejected the peace offer of a cigarette, formally returned to his seat and did not forget to straighten his red armband. Half a minute later, Hang began to laugh aloud, her laughter punctured by mixed comments '*c'est drole*', '*c'est comique*', '*parfaite!*'.

I got up and left.

He also left. The first grapes were too bitter. A few days later Hang felt sorry and went to visit him at his house. He received her at the door, waved his hand, 'It's nothing, it's unimportant', muttered a semi-cryptic comment, 'I've been busy', and coldly turned and went inside.

And he was busy. For six long months, Quang the dwarf left the world of those who were no better than him except for a few lousy hormones. He set out to pursue his goal, the only baggage his huge determination. He started training, in the track-and-field world where crossbars combined with human determination to create new persons. He searched for the creator within. His second birth must improve on the imperfect product of the first. The great experiment with a deficient length. Nobody could imagine the effort of his stubborn challenge to fate.

Exactly six months later, he again faced those hormone-sufficient humans, now 126 centimetres from head to heel. One hundred and twenty-five plus one. Six months for a centimetre, convincing evidence of human determination, thrown in the faces of the superficially endowed such as Hang and her six followers. If necessary, the dwarf star could invest another sixty times six months – thirty years – and be over a metre eighty, able to bend down to laugh at the noses of his little Asian compatriots. But he had other goals, more pressing and more worthy. The first test had been successful. There was no need to prove the point any further.

I received twenty roses and a very non-dwarf declaration of love. I received all the remnants of people's unfulfilled ambitions, unsatisfied desires. The world sees me as its dumping place. Who do I have? Me, the reluctant youngest of the family, the world's mute snail, a humble bottomless bin.

I don't know when Quang the dwarf changed tack and began to direct his attention towards me. From that lakeside evening when I got up and left, leaving behind the francophonic laughter of Hang's friends? Or three years earlier, when he began to sense in me a heart that beat to the same tempo, even if only because it beat inside another body of the same size, 125 centimetres? Or perhaps from the time when my parents hinted that 'each pot has its own matching lid'? I am indeed a bunch of grapes within his reach. I have said that human desires are so rarely met, perhaps once in every two or three hundred years, and it must be a meeting of flesh and bone and of heart and mind, a far cry from a simple matter of matching the shapes of lids and pots and pans. Hang ran away from that rare but great and demanding love; she followed those matching geometrical shapes, enclosing circles without escape, poor sister Hang.

'I love you, Hoai, but we can not allow love to overcome our rational thoughts. I have to go: the urgent needs of the revolution are calling. The expansionist enemies are invading us. We can't sit still while they trample our country. In two years' time, on this same day, I will return and ask for your hand. I will return.'

He disappeared from my window, the miraculous *fata morgana*. The brave tin soldier set off, laughed at the universities perching on the four pillars of Intellect, Morality, Strength and Aesthetics, at the paper castles and their greying theories, and said to them: 'Wait there, I will return.'

From the frontier, he sent me his letters twice a week in numbered envelopes, the left-hand corner marked with *from the front*, the right-hand corner *to the girl at home*. I continued to sit by my window, releasing cotton threads to connect my yeasty brown world to the battlefront on the border: a deserted township, burning houses surrounded by mountains dotted with checkpoints, both ours and the enemy's. In that chaos was Hoai's fiancé, carrying a rifle taller than himself. I was worried and anxious; I used up all my mother's black-and-white cotton threads and started to use Hang's coloured embroidery threads. War was an incomprehensible fate; it did not depend on me, or on him. He was happy to choose war as a fire to light his own life. In his letters war took on a man's face, bright and brave. I was worried, as in truth the face of war was more like a woman's, pained and anxious.

At one minute to zero hour of the twenty-ninth of March 1981 he appeared under my window, 126 centimetres framed in a blue pullover, yellow trousers ironed into two stiff columns, and a new pair of sand-shoes, their whiteness accentuating the red of his socks. At precisely zero hour on her twenty-second birthday little Hoai received her first proposal. From a fiancé who never knew that the colour of my eyes changed from yellow to blue and grey, who had never heard the whispers of my ten fingers each singing a different tune, had never breathed the virginal smell of a little girl who stole the forbidden fruit from her father's garden before becoming a woman. A fiancé who had nothing to place at my feet except dizzying memories of my full-moon twin sister and the self-imposed challenges that drained the energy of the poor dwarf star.

I had been waiting by my window for somebody to come and kidnap me. He opened his arms at zero hour and five minutes, the single naked light of the brewery's security post the sole witness of this sacred moment. Everything whirled around me; a dark red sea swelled, reached my chest, my chin and then engulfed me. I began to float, gave a happy cry and drifted into a wonderfully deep embryonic sleep, rocking on crests of red waves, blood that you shed once and forever, lulled by the soothing lullaby of the public water tap. He was truly a miraculous *fata morgana*, attached to me, embracing me, a desert snail.

Funerals and weddings: the arts of deception of the adult world that I couldn't understand.

Mother got up and carried me comatose to my bed. Rubbing me with oil she said: 'Oh dear, she must have caught a terrible chill.' Father also got up. 'Dear oh dear, more trouble, when is it going to end, my God?' And angrily slammed the window.

The following morning, when I heard the

unmistakable sound of Quang clearing his throat, I screamed, covered my head with my blanket and rolled into a corner of the bed trembling. He came in, looked at Che for a moment and then quietly turned on his heels and left.

He never came again. How the aura of that dwarf star contracted or expanded, what cosmic signals beckoned that mini celestial body, I do not know. He remained single, the incumbent Secretary of the local Group and unsure whether he ought to take the position of chairman of the People's Committee at sub-district level or to stay with the Group to become its Secretary at District level. In the seven years since then he has managed to complete two degrees in foreign languages, settling the debt of that francophonic laughter, one in-service university degree, settling the score against the universities, and he now wears a pair of tortoise-shell glasses. Each day he works fourteen hours at the office, touch-typing at incredible speed, resolving complaints of all kinds, organising meetings and, in addition, playing sport. On big occasions he even helps in preparing and putting up large posters.

When Hang turned up to register her marriage he personally supervised the procedure. His sad red eyes stared at the nib of his pen, which, at a stroke, would forever close a romantic chapter of a dwarf. When finished, he shook their hands and in an even voice read out the appropriate congratulations, but the gaze of his burning eyes remained fixed to and struggled helplessly against the second top button of my sister's blouse.

CHAPTER 10
Untitled

There are those born to belong to each other. They recognise each other by the signals of fireflies, defying the normal explanations offered by philosophy, morality, aesthetics, sociology, mythology, and sexology, those theories that cocoon self-destructive humans.

There are those born to belong to each other. They know that they belong to one another and they never hurry, immune to the modern disease that drives humans relentlessly onward like pawns that can only move one way: forward to a dead end.

There are those born to belong to each other.

They believe in each other and are not afraid, while all around them fear forms into mental and emotional fortresses whose sole function is defense, or crystallises into millions of tumours, growing, intersecting, and blocking out primal human urges.

There are those born to belong to each other. I and he, the girl at the window and the man outside.

CHAPTER 11
The Funeral

The funeral of the writer regarded as the greatest, the most imposing mountain in the relatively flat landscape of modern Vietnamese literature, took place on the summer solstice at the head office of the Combined Associations of Literature and Arts on Tran Hung Dao Street. He lived to be nearly eighty, the latter half of his life an echo of the glorious first half. To use his own tone of disdain: he died at the age of thirty but his burial took place forty or fifty years later. My father's collection, of course, did not spare him. I read his complete works three times, at three or four-year intervals; each time they

seemed more irrelevant. Nobody of my generation read him, but everybody mentioned him in
tones of reverence. That is to say his place had
been fixed in our encyclopaedias. My sister
Hang could only scan a few lines of his work
before starting to yawn, but she was very keen to
drag me along to pay our respects to the
deceased. One of her recent lovers had met him
at an artists' drinking session somewhere and felt
that he could not live the rest of his life in peace
unless he came to farewell his older friend. Yes,
everyone was a friend of this writer. His astrol-
ogy chart was strongest in its 'slavery sector'.

When they took little Hon away, I hid under
the bed. Not once did I look at her coffin or shed
one drop of farewell tears.

The centre of a closed circle, the sharp point
of a brutal compass: the inescapable point of
death for each person. I do not regard death as
real. I have never put my name forward as a
candidate for death. Birth and death, both of
them are outside your control. I am only
concerned with real existence: the absolute
value between those extremes. Within this finite
span, most humans scurry around filling up
time's footprints towards death. Others take
their time and leisurely watch their own gliding
towards the end. As for me, I fill the span
between birth and death with a constant search
for tenderness. What else can confirm that I
have existed between birth and death?

How the deceased writer had managed his
span of over two-thirds of a century, I don't
know. But now it was difficult to find him for the

sea of flowers – flowers respectfully sent from the Literature and Arts Association, respectfully from Journal such and such, Factory flowers, Organising Committee flowers – for the formal funereal suits walking with the robotic movements of chess pieces, for the incense burning indoors competing with the 41-degree heat outside in the vast summer solstice atmosphere, for the throng of cars and bicycles lining up to sign the register of condolence, for the chaotic random camera flashes, for the appropriate facial expressions, wax mannequins and so on.

Her lover held Hang's hand, she mine. Like in the game of *dragons and snakes* we wound our way through the crowd that spilled over into the street. Curious cyclists stopped and craned their necks to watch, hoping to receive a tonic for their tired, bored existence. Sightseers, ticket scalpers operating outside the August Revolution Cinema without anything to do between screenings, an army of *cyclo* drivers seeking a fare ... and he, the man without a face, leading a group of his species.

Oh, the great drawing power of the centre of a closed circle, death as a red-hot magnet, utterly illogical, lying naked under the terrible clear blue of a summer solstice sky.

Little Hon died on a cold and bitter winter's day. To the last minute her lips remained bright like two little glowing embers lost in an otherwise grey and cold world.

Finally, drenched in sweat, we got inside the forecourt of the head office of the Combined Association of Literature and Arts and came to a long table draped in a white tablecloth, the registration table for participating delegations. The woman in black sitting behind the table looked at us, dragons and snakes, still holding onto each other, politely smiled and asked: 'And which organisation are you from?' My sister Hang belonged to the National Library, her lover to Technoimport, I to myself – a curious mix. I'm not sure how we escaped from that table. Before I recovered, I found in front of me a huge wreath, behind me an even greater one, wreaths everywhere, beautiful shields. Hang and her Technoimport man had evaporated without trace in the dense midsummer heat. Where had the dragon head and the snake body gone, leaving me, the bony tail, sandwiched between someone else's wreaths? When alive, the writer used to discuss the finer things of life such as rare flowers, exotic tea, delicate incense and exquisite food, things like that. I had heard that he was quite a connoisseur. What an appropriate funeral! When alive, little Hon only longed for understanding, gentleness, a soft, kind word each morning, a shared look, an encouraging smile, a caressing hand to help the flesh drift into secure sleep. Is there a funeral appropriate to such primal longings?

Lost but safe among the fortress of flowers, I inched my way towards the remains of the famous writer. One by one, each delegation took their place in front of the funeral parlour, checked themselves for the last time – clothes, hair and mind – before going in. Again, one by one each delegation emerged from the parlour, a mysterious black box that swallowed people at one end and spat out wax mannequins at the other. The wreath in front of me had gone inside. Flowers in front went in first, flowers behind followed, and here I was, caught in between, without flowers, without a group, without letters of introduction, without registration. The organising committee gestured for the next delegation to come in. I stepped inside. Hundreds of eyes left the resplendent coffin and fixed on me. Cameras, raised by the force of habit, froze in mid-air, their blackness appropriate to the serious atmosphere of the funeral. A crowd drifted on the foundation of slow funereal music. Immediately I began to classify them: Homosapiens-A Homosapiens-Z, ample faces and hungry faces, and those without a face. After my task was done, I bade farewell to the famous writer, although a stranger to me, and left, leaving behind a pool of sweat on the marble floor, a stunned organising committee, and the embarrassed and bewildered relatives of the deceased.

Hang and the Technoimport man greeted me at the gate. They had dropped their plan to pay their respects, since our status was somewhat irregular; nevertheless they had managed to write a few lines in the 'visitors' impressions' book, signing as 'loyal readers'. I am prepared to believe that Mr Technoimport will forever remain loyal to the memory of the artists' drinking session of that one day and his loyalty will live on for generations to come. As for Hang, she is perfectly capable of being loyal to whatever she does not possess.

It was the only funeral that I had witnessed in my twenty-nine years. It was on the summer solstice, the temperature reached forty-one degrees, the sky was infinitely blue and dense with sunlight.

Several days later my sister Hang brought home some snippets of gossip. The rumour was that on the day of the funeral a young girl of about thirteen or fourteen attended by herself. She did not cry, did not laugh, she brought no flowers, no incense, she simply came and left, quite possibly an unfortunate illegitimate love child.

CHAPTER 12
The Selection

To the last, my sister Hang did not know whom to choose out of the three hundred satellites circling around her, mayflies infatuated by the moon. She was then twenty-five – beautiful, sad, difficult to understand.

At first she trusted her lot to fate. 'It wouldn't matter, they are all the same, don't you think?' Peals of laughter. 'Let's draw lots.' She asked me to write the men's names, as I pleased, on three hundred pieces of paper. Three hundred times I wrote the same initial, Ph. She slowly brushed her hair, carefully put on her make-up, then came to sit in front of the three hundred solutions.

'Well, let's see what this open bazaar brings,' she said and calmly picked one, shuddered a little, folded it, returned it to the pile and said softly, 'Let's try again.' Second time, third time, her ivory face went paler with each draw. She buried her face in her two lovely hands with beautiful long fingers, sat in silence, and finally stood up and put a match to the three hundred devil-possessed pieces of paper. Three hundred Phs fused into a fire, unique, ceaselessly burning, shackling her life no matter where she goes and what she does.

The poet was a dove-eyed, quiet and innocent man who would argue one on one with highly placed people yet would concede defeat even to a three-year-old. Other men, in contrast, were like boisterous roosters crowing atop sewer drains, life's surreal sewer drains that sucked away all needs and dreams.

They recognised each other at a three-way intersection during rush hour. The poet and the Moon Goddess, frozen in their daydreams, caused a huge traffic jam never before witnessed in the history of the city's public transport. The full complement of the city's traffic police had to be mobilised; it took three hours to clear the traffic, and they still stood there, the indefinite conversation between two palms. The poet was poor, working as a builder's labourer during the day and writing poetry at night. His face, haggard and twisted by emotion, was more passionate than that of a prince prepared to set his whole vast dominion, on which the sun never sets, at the foot of the beautiful Moon Goddess.

Hang could never have a relationship with any man for longer than three months without a union of the flesh. The door, forced open that disastrous day, could not be closed again. She discussed making love as mother would the Sunday shopping. The only exception was Ph the poet, passionate but distant. Sitting next to him, gazing eye to eye, her delicate fingers timid in his callused hands, breathing the manly scent from his lips in order to imagine, just to imagine, a deep kiss – that was enough for her to feel a softening sensation, a melting, a falling into a vast, unconfined sea of pleasure.

'They are all the same, don't you think, but he doesn't belong ... Oh, I'm afraid ... I'm afraid ...' The same centuries-old cry. As I have said, Hang ran away from this kind of rare but great and demanding love; she searched for those matching shapes, concentric circles closing in without escape, poor sister Hang.

Acting as if the lottery – drawn three hundred times with only one possible outcome – had never occurred, Hang decided to hold a competition to select a husband. The first condition of this competition was to find her: a childhood game of hide-and-seek extended to adulthood, a journey back to point zero, where the y and x axes meet, a journey back to embryonic slumber. On the fixed day, Hang disappeared without trace. Two hundred and ninety-nine suitors (Ph did not participate, just as he would eschew all competitions) searched for her down all the streets and lanes of the city. They searched in restaurants and dance halls, clubs and theatres, parks, pagodas and the lake; they searched from tourist shops to public toilets, wharves to stations, park benches to boardrooms; they looked under the hats of each pedestrian in the street, under bushes with magnifying glasses, and some even obtained special passes to enter the infamous Hanoi Hilton jail: a woman like my sister might do the craziest of things.

By the time the deadline approached, the city had been mangled and mauled by 598 searching hands. Five hundred and ninety-eight eyes searched every corner of the disturbed body of Hanoi. Their collective search was ant-tight, but their desired Moon Goddess had disappeared. Defeated and hopeless, they gathered under my window to face the final moment.

All this time my twin sister was sobbing in a little attic room filled with twilight dimness, thick with cheap but strong incense, and full of indefinable smells. The occupant, sex uncertain, sat quite still somewhere in the room, occasionally blessing this working-class hell with a couple of grunts in a hoarse and severe voice. 'If you want a husband, take a husband. I see no happy star in your marriage sector.' Hang sobbed on, not once did she think of the 299 false slaves of love out there, energetic ants aggressively searching every nook and cranny. Enthusiastic and productive, children of the industrial age, they would frantically continue to search, to long for the perfect, only to step finally on one another's feet, trip over their own feet, become dazzled by their own images and never be able to leave their own dark shadows, able only to look without seeing, to search without finding, and to complain continually about their futile efforts. She chose that attic, its challenge and monotony, knowing that they wouldn't come near its dark and powerful forces. Only one person knew where she was – the quiet poet with deep dark eyes. The poet and the Moon Goddess never needed to make arrangements to meet as they always knew where to find each other when the need was strong enough.

Hang lay in that attic and longed for him, but Ph did not arrive.

She had often wanted him at the most unusual places and absurd times – at midnight in the bomb shelter built in 1972, at dawn on the banks of the Red River leading to the suburbs, or at noon in the middle of a stadium – and he had always come to her, as calmly as if he were carrying out the terms of a simple contract, never asking questions, never explaining his miraculous telepathic sense. Right now only he would know where she was, but Hang had burnt his name three hundred times, had sold herself in a competition in which Ph refused to take part. What's the use of telepathy? What's the use of the firefly signals? The game of hide-and-seek had finished. She had to return to the ants out there.

Under my window they were waiting, some sitting down, some standing up; their faces varied with the intensity of their longing. Then in a noisy explosion, all 299 of them, pushing and shoving, rushed towards her when she appeared from her secret hiding place. They kicked, shoved, fell, tripped over each other, some tackled others with elbows, some ran between others' legs, but only ten made it. Ten winners, making a simultaneous record, rushed forward and at exactly the same time knelt down in front of my sister, each taking hold of one of her long tapering fingers. She wondered whether she ought to marry all ten of them together, or allow them to take their turn, each for one year.

The second round of the competition was to see which of the ten would be the earliest with their offerings. On the fixed date, with their bags of gifts big and small, the five Mountain Gods and the five Water Gods converged at the same time, at precisely zero hour in the morning.

The Horticultural Engineer brought flowers and herbs, those in season and those out of season. The expert in the Foreign Exchange and Money Market displayed a whole collection of notes: roubles, yen, marks and dollars, Vietnamese notes of 1975 and 1978, and proudly displayed them as one would in the children's game of pebbles and sticks. The surgeon brought a complete, perfect anatomical chart of the human conscience. The Master of Arts in Archaeology held out a jar of indeterminate age, red cellophane hermetically sealing aeons of the past within it, offering thousands of dead time-tissues at the feet of the proud My Nuong. The expert in home economics brought a flock of huge chickens, their nests full of eggs, plus a herd of pigs, both real and piggy banks. The architect arrogantly arrived with nothing, bringing with him only his talents and the promise to provide a comprehensive master plan for everything, from cities to every kind of building: eateries, residences, love-nests, studies and retreats. The official from the Foreign Affairs Department offered a globe of solid gold engraved with miraculous diverging routes towards destinations in the civilised world. The office worker pushed along a filing cabinet, its drawers full of timetables and other trivia, offering a life that's boring, predictable but safe. Even the humble lottery agent threw all he had – stacks of unsold lottery tickets – into this gamble of love. And finally him, the man without a face, bringing with him nothing but his destructive disease which would reduce humanity to a faceless common denominator.

It was a masculine harem of the era of upper-class 'marriages of equals'. They all converged under my window at zero hour, not one of them half a foot quicker than the other, creating such a jostling racket that their offers swallow up the owners. Many years later the neighbours still complained about that terrible day of groom selection. Fortunately, there was none of the mythological revenge between the mighty rival Water God and Mountain God. At this impasse, my sister decided to open the final round of the competition: the winner would be the one who could guess what her greatest wish was.

A hush descended on the prospective princes. They looked into each other's eyes, as none of them dared to look into my sister's fossilised gaze. They peered at each other, searching deeper into their own souls and those of their companions, examining themselves from all angles, hoping to find the secret dream of the woman they so desired to possess.

I laughed at them tearing their hair out. My sister did not know herself what she wanted, so how could there be a 'back-page answer' to this puzzle? Like a ship incapable of finding its direction, running away from something unknown, searching for the unknown, once again, this last time she trusted her fate to whatever shore came randomly into sight, gliding by habit, only because not gliding was impossible.

The guesses came flying thick and fast into the emerging rays of the rising sun. They flew at random, forming themselves into clouds of multi-coloured soap bubbles, obscuring the weak early rays of sunlight, and causing the neighbours to complain, 'Why is dawn so late today?'

– Genuine French perfume.
– Freedom.
– Life-long wealth.
– Power.
– To be able to live as you wish.
– A trip overseas.
– Immortality.
– A holiday in Da Lat.
– To be world famous.

Hang continued to shake her head. The first and final wish that any human can make is for happiness, but as happiness is only a feeling, what can guarantee it, what can measure, compare or analyse it? What magic can create its birdlike soaring feeling, its animal-like earthiness?

At that moment, a voice called out:

– I know. You wish to have a child.

Hang gave a start. Life suddenly returned to her fossilised eyes. She narrowed her eyes a little and smiled. The Foreign Affairs official did not seem too bad for a prospective father – good-looking, strong and healthy, of good breeding. She took a step forward and extended her hand to him in the silence of the early morning – the absolute silence when everyone's hearts skipped a beat and then returned to beating normally, except for the heart of the poor lottery agent, which stopped forever. Paying no attention to that tragedy, the couple went straight to the registry office, where Quang the dwarf worked day and night.

The groom, still stunned by such happiness grasped in the nick of time, did not notice the way the gaze of the government official was caught in and struggled helplessly against the second top button of the young wife's blouse.

CHAPTER 13
The Wedding

The wedding followed immediately. The place was set up with partitions and screens, decorated with dubious copies of Russian paintings, and temporarily extended out onto the street with marquees, tables and chairs. People drank and socialised, received and returned social debts, made acquaintances and reforged long-forgotten family ties, showed off their cosmetic beauty, clothes and wealth, or simply killed time under my window for a day and a night.

Father and mother agonised, caught in the tension between two social rules. On the one hand the behaviour expected of a clean and scrupulous cadre's family did not allow for a lavish show; on the other hand an 'equal marriage' demanded that they must not lose face by being seen as less well-off than the groom's family, shining representatives of the upper class to whom going overseas was as common as a shopping trip and to whom the only sport worth playing was tennis.

My second oldest brother, a recent computing graduate from a Russian university, became my father's trump card. Russian folk-music, vodka and cigarettes were reserved for the head table. All his Russian-trained friends were mobilised, men and women stiffly bound in ill-designed Western clothes who had lost the precision of their speech, unable to find the exact Vietnamese words for each situation.

In contrast, my wayward brother Hac, now a gambling racketeer, and his addicted gamblers who lived off the black market or hustled food stamps around state-run food stores, were banished, strictly forbidden at the door. Even the trusty pipe, normally inseparable from father, and the rickety chairs, inseparable from my family, were given their marching orders and evacuated to the neighbours'. A *coup d'état* took place in father's bookcase: the criteria for prominence changed from substance to thickness. I could not help laughing when I saw the novel *Buoi chiêu* by a certain little-known Nguyen Van Quai boldly taking the prominent place that had once been reserved for Lermontov and Neruda. The adult world's art of deception. But this world did not discard me, a deformed and useless being, an ugly burden. Perhaps because of some vague reason such as humanistic concern, that world accepted me with a sigh.

I don't believe that my sister Hang cares all that much about that world either, a world so formal and devoid of integrity and love, which denies people's most basic and primal yearnings. On her wedding day, her eyes remained fossilised, her face beautiful, sad and inscrutable. She did not participate in the tacky proceedings around her, as if it were someone else's wedding. They draped a resplendent wedding dress over her, pressed a lovely virginal bouquet of flowers into her hands and admired her. Some swooned, some froze open-mouthed, captivated by her arresting beauty. She, on the other hand, was quite oblivious of the forceful ripples left in her wake. Absentmindedly, guided by other people, like a self-righting doll which had lost its capacity to regain its balance, she would lean this way to acknowledge father's introduction to a man wearing a wide tie, 'Come and greet Uncle ... Yes, her husband works with the Foreign Affairs Department. Just returned from Singapore ...', or lean that way to give a plastic smile to the camera held by a busy little man who darted here and there like a clown, not remembering anyone and not forgetting anyone, an ideal attitude to have at weddings.

Half an hour before the groom's family was due to arrive, Hang went to her room, saying that she wished to be alone, breaking away from the women crowding around her in the name of friendship, who were determined to straighten a lock of hair here, to re-clip a flower there, to add a little padding to the already perfect bust of the bride. I crawled through under everyone's legs to her room, hid myself quietly behind the pile of cosmetic accessories, and mournfully watched my twin sister holding her head in her two beautiful hands. The fire of the three hundred talismans named Ph had flared again. I prayed for an explosion to blow the roof away and for the poet to descend and rescue the Moon Goddess away from this world of loveless marriage.

But what happened was that the door opened, almost soundlessly.

A strange man came in, dressed exactly like Gary Cooper in *High Noon*, but without the gun. He walked in self-assuredly, closed the door behind him with his foot, folded his arms across his chest and stood leaning against the wall, a long cigar in his lips. Hang's face turned a deathly white.

'You recognise me?' The stranger came close, lifted her chin and said, as if to himself, 'God, you are even more beautiful now than you were.'

Hang brushed his hand away, turning her face aside, also just like in the movie.

'It's me, it's Hoang.'

Silence.

Teacher Hoang got down on his knees, his performance on the same artistic par as Gary Cooper's.

Hang spoke in a weak whisper, 'Go away, go away.'

'Why? Why? Eight long years ... I left home because you slapped my face.'

'Please, just go away.'

'I left everything, career, friends. Everyone thought that I had perished! Simply because of a slap on the face. Eight long uncertain years, many brushes with death, jail, hunger, criminals, but I never lost the wish to return, and now I have. Look at me! Am I not good enough for you now?'

'What do you want?'

'I want you! I want to take you away from your stupid husband,' Hoang said with a laugh.

'And how would you do that?' the normal tone returned to my sister's voice, tinged with her usual sarcasm.

Teacher Hoang gave his own arrogant laugh: 'I possess everything that any man of my age can hope to have. The young fool, the romantic Teacher Hoang of old has died, my dear, and what remains now is Hoang the Boss, Hoang the Ice-King. Isn't that enough to repay a slap in the face?'

'I've forgotten what happened. Just go away, and don't bother me any more. Please go away.' Her sudden pleading excited his self-confidence. He stood up in a manly way. It was true that no trace of his former self was left. There was no trace of the lovesick weakling in the new man, who looked weathered and sophisticated, who pounded his heels on the floor as he paced, a habit acquired on the day he became the boss of the whole business network of ice-making and distributing in tropical Saigon.

Hoang shook his head. 'I have not forgotten. Your hand left a permanent welt on my cheek! Look here.' He removed his checked shirt. 'This is a scar, that is a tattoo – you are scared, aren't you? – but these marks are nowhere near as indelible as your slap to my face. You gave yourself to me. And apparently I left you with something. Where is it?'

'What are you talking about?' my sister hissed savagely.

'Oh dear. Perhaps your idiotic husband doesn't know about our affair. Let me enlighten him, then. Now, listen here ... ' He sweetly approached my sister.

I did not need to jump out to intervene because just then the door again burst open, accompanied by much crying and yelling. It was a scrawny dishevelled woman, holding tight to her chest a funeral wreath with an eighteen by twenty-four portrait framed in black, the portrait of the lottery agent. She screamed, 'You killed my husband! Oh, heaven and earth listen to this, she killed my husband! I will cut open your face, you little slut of a bitch!' Then she broke into a sobbing cry 'Oh, my darling, you died, you left me with little children and no support!' Behind her a baffled crowd blocked the doorway. The woman paused when she saw Hoang standing there but then continued her advance, without ceasing her wailing. The modern Rivares took less than three seconds to figure out the scandal; his eight years in exile from romanticism and Victor Hugo had not been a waste.

'Come on, stop it!' he said, and stepped in

front of the woman, firmly gripping her wrists. A razor blade dropped to the floor and he ground it with the heel of his shoe. Holding the woman with one hand, he reached into his pocket with the other and took out a bundle of money which he held under her gasping, panting mouth, saying through gritted teeth 'Is this enough?' Her eyes flashed in cunning assessment; the deceased husband had not been worth a cent. But she looked at the money with contempt, gathered her strength and started to wail again.

Teacher Hoang smiled contemptuously and slowly removed a ring with a huge stone from his little finger. Placing it in his palm on top of the money, he flashed it under her nose. The two antagonists stared at one another for a second or so and then the woman stopped crying, dropped the wreath, grabbed up the ring, clutched the bundle of money and stuffed it down her corset, and half-ran out of the door. The crowd parted to make way for her, their shocked eyes fixed on the ice-king.

They parted again, wave-like, to make way for someone else, a well-built young man, his beard not quite covering the long scar on his face, his hair closely cropped, a loose American jacket flapping over a pair of faded jeans: my brother Hac. He grabbed Hoang by the shirt-front before the nostalgic love soapie could continue, the story about a slap on the face, the story of the transformation from a second-rate teacher to a hero of the ice age.

'What the hell are you doing here?' Hac yelled with wall-trembling force. 'Get out of my sight, you scum. Here, take this and piss off! Piss off!' The bundle of money and the ring with its huge stone suddenly appeared in his hand as if by a miracle. My brother pressed them to Hoang's face and at the same time dragged him towards the door. The woman fearfully merged into the crowd.

'Hey, hey, hang on, my friend. There seems to have been some misunderstanding!'

'Misunderstanding or not, please leave. And go quickly! Don't think that your money will fix everything!'

'Ah, who do I have the pleasure of talking to?' Hoang's tone remained polite and sweet.

'Hac's the name. Who wouldn't know my face? Just piss off!' Hac pointed to the scar on his face and patted it with his palm. I must admit that he looked quite extraordinary.

'You and your family really ought to thank me. The scandal brewing just now ...' Hoang tactfully rubbed the tip of his shoe on the ground where fragments of the razor blade glittered in the light.

'Shut up!' Hac again grabbed his shirt-front. 'Don't talk money to me! As brother of that crazy girl I don't need your type! Money? Look at this!' He flung his arms out like a magician. Hundreds of colourful notes fluttered down like butterflies, hitting teacher Hoang and the hypnotised crowd in the face and then settling in a pile at my brother's feet. Hoang nodded in impressed admiration.

'Look at it! Take a good look, then piss off with the miserable loot you've just learnt to pinch from other people's pockets. You'd have been better off continuing mouthing old lessons at the class lectern. You think your money will fix everything? You're a miserable sod!'

Teacher Hoang began to grit his teeth. 'Look here, my friend. Don't carry on like that in front of women. Watch your manners. I'm at least your father's or your uncle's age.'

'A bastard is a bastard at any age,' my brother retorted.

As Hoang replied 'OK, just you wait,' a young girl with white skin, blue eyes and an aquiline nose, a perfect mixed-blood product, came running in. 'Oh Hoang, my darling! Why did you leave me by myself? What's happening here, darling?'

His nineteen-year-old lover, of 50 per cent Texas extraction, who had lived off nightclubs in Saigon from the age of ten, who worshipped the owner of the ice business as she would anyone who could rise above the terrible struggle for food, money, power, status, suddenly found herself in Hanoi at this half-Eastern European half-Vietnamese village market wedding.

Abandoned by Hoang as soon as they got to Hanoi, a little disoriented at first, she quickly made use of her unusual beauty and uncommon torch-singer's voice. Encouraged by a growing crowd of admiring men, she began to sing and dance to the acclaim of the fascinated spectators. In less than half an hour her deep blue eyes, half closed as any singer's would be, had scanned all the faces around her. Disappointed by what she saw, finding not one interesting face among the hundreds whose essence was obedience and acceptance, the dancer, singer and professional lover suddenly remembered her owner, went in search, and found him in this spectacular situation.

Who knows what that trio – ice-king, numbers-man and dancer – would have done next if not for the inevitable appearance of the mini excla-mation mark, Quang the dwarf. Throughout the wedding he had hidden in a corner, not clinking his glass, not blowing cigarette smoke seriously, not parading himself, his time-defying face hunched over his knees, an insignificant face so small that it almost sank without trace between his two skinny knees, his fierce burning eyes peering out, not leaving Hang for a second, full of gloom, full of ominous tidings.

He rose in the middle of the field of battle like a mushroom, contemptuously flashed his Red Flag Youth Brigade badge, the trump card from that earlier lakeside evening, and requested 'All concerned present here, please follow me to the station to make a report. Your crimes are hideous: murder, devaluing socialist currency, disturbing public peace.' And behind him was the cold professional face of the second lieu-tenant of the local police.

The wedding had become a tragi-comedy, moving from scene one Hollywood, to scene two Kitsch, to scene three Underworld, to scene four Opera. The dwarf clown dominated centre-stage, forcing all the main characters into the wings.

I stopped praying for an explosion to blow up

the roof. Throughout the four scenes my twin sister had remained paralysed and mute, a crucified witness without the strength to lift the crown of thorns off her head.

No-one but I, the twin witness, could end this absurd drama with its final scene, the Harvest. I grew up like a second mushroom next to him. I knew that with my appearance, the mysterious power of the dwarf, of that absurd clown, would be deflated. His peculiar advantage turned to painful water trickling down his legs. The dwarf star's bright shining moment had ended. We looked at each other using the secret code of two stunted bodies, one created by the will of nature, the other by human will, and he turned away, not daring to face the twenty dry roses and the stack of letters in my hand '*from the front to the girl at home*'.

At that moment the firecrackers exploded, lovely and perfect, signalling the arrival of the groom carrying a solid gold globe. In a blink the stage cleared. Even the crowd of onlookers, indifferent yet ready to take sides if necessary, dispersed quickly. They receded like an outgoing tide, leaving me stranded on the desolate beach, a small lonely snail surrounded by tons of rubbish, glinting razor fragments, a funeral wreath bearing the portrait of the unfortunate lottery agent, twenty dry roses, letters and a pile of colourful money.

The end of something.

And Hang walked towards the exploding firecrackers, hoping to conceive a solid golden child. Children will be born out of this world,

the world of teacher Hoang who sold out Victor
Hugo for the ice business, of the dancer who
sold her body for passing whims, of lottery
agents trusting their lives to luck, of my brother
the gambling racketeer who turned his back on
culture, of the little dwarf clown, fanatic and
driven by an inferiority complex, of Moon
Goddesses who can not find their own balance
... What difference will my own dissension
make? Will it lead to a blossoming of
Homosapiens-As in the world? I had just ended
a terrible scene, an overture not inappropriate
for the wedding of my sister, a crazy woman
who had let slip from her hands all capacity to
control and build happiness for herself. But
there was a limit to my own capacity too.
Something had come to an end but nothing
much had changed.

I began to doubt the significance and the
meaning of my dissension.

The wedding continued. The dancer sang and
danced. A table was prepared for the wife and
children of the lottery agent. The groom poured
vodka and clinked his glass with teacher Hoang,
brother Hac and Quang the dwarf. The adult
world's art of deception.

Father and mother had tried to hide me in a
corner so as not to have to introduce me to the
guests, offer explanations, feel pain, and most
importantly, not to have to blame each other in
front of so many guests. But my sister Hang
found me. Before stepping into the wedding car
with its usual decoration – a pretty doll sitting
with its legs spread wide – she held me tight and

cried, her tears soaking my pigtailed hair. 'I'm afraid, I'm afraid ...'

My hair again felt feverish.

CHAPTER 14
The Gamble

Name:	VU BA HAC	NGUYEN HOANG
Alias:	Bearded Hac	Hoang Van
Occupation:	Gambling business	Ice business
Position:	Proprietor	Proprietor
Education:	Year seven (discontinued)	Teacher
Peculiarities:	Long scar on the face	Tattoos on chest and arm
Love life:	Free	Married, numerous lovers
Personal career:	Left school at thirteen, sold	Left history at thirty, lived as a

ice-cream,	drifter, wrote
scalped tickets,	poetry, traded
drove a *cyclo*,	in photographic
joined the army,	paper, traded
deserted, joined	in second-
the army again,	hand goods,
discharged from	imprisoned,
the army, owner	released from
of numbers	prison, owner of
game.	ice business.

Voice: Bass   Tenor

The two proprietors faced each other. They sat on the floor covered with the red remnants of firecrackers, in front of them a deck of cards dealt into three piles with one pile discarded. A four-handed game would have been more interesting but nobody wanted to be involved in the savage struggle between these two. Quang the dwarf came up but teacher Hoang brushed him aside: 'Go and blow your nose, little kid.' Hac shooed off another innocent would-be contender, my brother Hung, 'Listen, brains, this is not for you, too tough for you to digest.' Quang the dwarf cursed: 'You just wait, one day you'll have all the time in the world to gamble with death.' Hung smiled timidly, his mind automatically beginning to draft a computer program to configure the infinite permutations of the cards.

They sat facing each other on the floor covered with shreds of red firecracker. The bride and groom had left without looking back. People began to clean up, saving un-eaten food and drink, un-used smiles and platitudes, un-settled relationships and social debts, and heaping them up to create new table spreads for latecomers. They opened the gift envelopes and carefully compared name and status with the contents therein; nodding in appreciation or sneering with contempt, they calculated in silence. The wedding had entered its auditing phase. Apart from cash, every other gift was a round vanity mirror. Twenty-four identical mirrors to wish the bride and groom a life of twenty-four full, round hours a day. Each morning the Moon Goddess would be able to look at herself in two dozen mirrors. Wonderful!

They sat facing each other on the floor covered with the red remnants of firecrackers, the deck of cards dealt into three piles with one pile discarded, doubling-up their bets each time, the two non-believers, having had everything in life, ultimately to reject it all, except for the feeling that only wealth and unfettered freedom combined can bring. They sat cross-legged, motionless and immovable, their whole beings engrossed in the progression of the cards, which began with the ugly three of spades, advanced, odd, odd, stopped, a black pair, a red pair, levelled off, then advanced, advanced to an impromptu card of two, then a unique flush from three to nine, a cruel endgame. The ring with its huge stone passed from the ice-king to the numbers-racket man. The American jacket on the body of the numbers-man moved to the somewhat thinner and more elegant body of the ice-king. Their fortunes ebbed and flowed. Baiting, trapping, they circled each other in a dizzying vortex of change. There were times when Hac was left with just his underpants. There were times when teacher Hoang was down to his last cigar. Each would lose nearly everything to the other only to calmly win it back, plus more in this infinite, unending gamble between the two cold, steely brains; the game itself was as chilling as the nocturnal laughter of the two players.

They would have continued to sit there forever, from the time the newlywed couple left to the time the same couple had children and grandchildren, from wedding season to funeral season; they would have sat there through aeons and climate changes. Fate was to make my brother meet teacher Hoang once more, to sit with him once more, but unfortunately in a place not covered by a red carpet of spent firecrackers; with the curse of Quang the dwarf hanging in the air. But now they were involved in the last game, winner takes all, to end their pointless eternal struggle. The final wager was the whole network of ice-making and distributing in tropical Saigon versus the complete gambling racket of temperate tea-drinking Hanoi.

'I have no regret. If I win I'll stay and move North. If I lose, *au revoir* to this damned medieval country.' That was Hoang's idea.

'I am different, I'll live where I was born, no choice. I'll take whatever life brings.' My brother's philosophy.

'My lucky star, don't abandon me,' Hoang joked, his hands in perpetual motion, shuffling, cutting and flicking the stiff, new cards.

The teacher dealt the cards, gained the lead, and from there advanced, doubled back, slowed down, let go. In perfect control and with a wonderful memory, he held onto his lead to the last minute without conceding it once to his opponent. Two cards remained in his hand, the three of clubs and the queen of spades, the advantage of holding the lead, the suit of spades yet to be played in this game. Teacher Hoang sat jiggling his knees impatiently, an old habit from his teaching time. Then, instead of playing the three of clubs, the finger of fate caused him to place the queen of spades on the floor covered with spent red firecrackers. His opponent coldly flicked down an ace, also of spades, and laid down a string of cards, all spades, full of black pips, black as the future of the now dethroned ice-king.

They shook hands, the deposed and the newly crowned.

'This means *au revoir* to this damned medieval place. Fate!' The re-made Rivares cracked a forced smile, but continued, 'My friend, luck is with you. You should seize it, let's have one final bet.'

'What do you have left to bet with?' My brother's curt tone sounded haughty, tinged with disdain.

'My last piece of precious property ... ha, ha ...' Hoang's eyes searched out the trembling dancer among the crowd watching the two gamblers. 'In any case I can't take her with me. Pirates, you know ...' With his hand Hoang made a stop sign that froze her to the spot.

'What would I do with that little puss?' my brother mumbled, not accepting yet not quite declining.

Again teacher Hoang dealt, gained the lead, advanced, doubled back, slowed down, let go. In perfect control and with a wonderful memory, he held onto the lead to the last minute without once conceding it to his opponent. Two cards remained in his hand, the seven of diamonds and the ace of hearts. Hoang paused to consider his cards, smiled, played the seven of diamonds to give the lead away, and smugly watched the bright red hearts on his supreme card of love, the suit of hearts yet to be played in this game. Hac played a pair, another pair, another pair, and yet another pair, followed by an unstoppable series of hearts from three to seven, then a tough, un-takeable black card, and just one step ahead of Hoang, played out his last card – a heart also – the modest nine of hearts.

Teacher Hoang stood up, his shoulders sagging like two huge inverted commas, and it was then that I saw for the first time a glimpse of his old self, the tired, accepting, powerless figure, the second-rate teacher, in this forty-something man. In the final minutes, just before he was to disappear for a long time from the centre stage only to reappear in another strange metamorphosis, he did not forget to conclude his Broadway play in the appropriate manner. He looked up to the sky and bemoaned the cruel twist of fate, laughed his shrill tenor laugh, took the dancer's hand to give her to Hac, stroked her smooth, 50 per cent Texan cheeks, said '*Adieu, baby,*' and theatrically turned on his heels. The farewell took place in an atmosphere full of red firecrackers, fulsome and perfect.

Teacher Hoang tried to escape from the country but failed.

The victor's prizes, one icy one sexy, spoils from that terrible game of cards, took turns to lead my family towards tragedy.

That's the way time and cards usually progress.

CHAPTER 15
Ph's Poetry

The morning is resplendent like a huge poem water flows between the two banks strewn with millions of mauve petals the colours of *bang lang* flowers range from violet to the brilliant white of flashing eyelashes every grove is a miracle the muffled singing voice follows you like traces of love I weave my gaze intently at the summer crossroads spell-bound by a twist of fate and frightened by the visual turmoil running anxiously through the ten fingers the larva of tomorrow through the empty ink-well the dreams of youth through the sexual atmosphere a city of dreams through the faces carved by

street kerbs and through the pollinating season
of the trees I sense by the total length of my
tangled web of neurones that the early April
sun-rays are leaving a white sediment on your
fragile fingers you escape the impasse of this
cryptic monologue when your soul reaches its
lowest ebb when the wellsprings of your
emotion dry out and when the sudden drought
hits you with immense disappointment you
escape along narrow streets clogged up with
peddling cyclists romantic canals clogged up
with paddling rowboats the whole world was
chasing you obsessed with violence which you
reject like the last surviving infatuated mohican
you live in your unique existence constructed
from the dust of hunger poverty and bliss I wish
you well on your street lake and market you
have captured patches of sunlight the colour of
fate which daily bring a slice of spectrum to
fossilised children who continue to wait for a
new great flood look there goes the ark of Noah
falling down from the outer rings of the eclipsed
sun the morning ceases to exist in the turning
wheel of the zodiac I trip over the meridian of
my elliptic journey leading to a fever of chaos
words flow in niagarian volumes to the trembling morning when you left my memories are
buried under stacks of masks but underneath
apocalyptic tides flow through an incoherent
series of thoughts which really are just a sob of
the intellect on this cruellest of days not just you
but a whole collection of beautiful girls of ha noi
have fallen for dreary boys roosters crowing
atop life's sewer but only you have burnt me in

my unpaginated manuscript which can be read either way depending on the how the fire consumes the words I have to face my own focal crisis as psychiatry's telescopes cannot be finely tuned to your face which changes its colour against the sky the colour of *bang lang* flowers pollen shed on the day of impregnation but as always I feel the energy drain I am like a modern ship whose propellers whirr when you glide smoothly alongside my thirst is oppressive my dry lips cry out but you shudder because my prose is flat like the morning beach the tide is dead in stillness but suddenly illusions come back life-like mirage of storms you frown and bite your lips to shreds the draft sketch is stilted laden with complexes the near extinct birds of paradise of timeless five dimensions and strange collections marked with roman numerals like the sudden biological changes of your soul which cried and died the 51:49 ratio in favour of those conditioned to express canned emotion you shed crocodile tears on the dying harmony of unrequited love you wiped your systolic murmur with the tattered rags that shield your life but you leave exposed the valves of your heart to show once and for all that you have left unaccomplished the golden interlude that precedes your masterpiece you regret that in your fitful slumber you killed the last mosquito on your forehead no more buzzing the laments that traverse your youth form the human bonding substance weak like the mauve petals flowing fast past the opaque optic lenses through the dizzying tonal registers which you descend tone by tone with such resplendent mornings of mythology then you will pass by and evaporate on the silica foundation of my poetry although at many crossroads I have relit extinguished fires hoping to reignite on your tired slender shoulders and in your vast open eyes a symbolic question the hesitation from that deep dark night has nurtured and launched the butterfly of love obliquely into the airspace of your magnetic field and an organic paradise will grow from illusions that were once abundant but devalued then another race will rise and the great symphony of creation will be born from the angry kiss of loss don't lose your focus don't look at yourself in the face of your watch as the hands will begin to move at full speed and the numerals will tick over in the frenzied rhythm of the modern discotheque in the rush of life in the crystals of salt deposited on the eight points of the finger webs of the wretched souls may those mauve flowers continue to fall in the season of remembrance as gently as I love you as if the terrifying mid-summer blue sky has shed bitterness and compassion on each step of yours so that my chest-wringing pain may cause my broken lines of verse to continue to cast their violet hue on your dress which flows towards infinity ...

CHAPTER 16
Model II

Many people have stood in the spot under my window where the wall's peeling stucco reveals patches of shoddy brickwork underneath, and where the ground sinks away like a fading note. In the future, when all that is now around me has become just an archaeological site, one of many layers covering a culture that rose and fell and sank forever beneath the earth, what will it reveal to future generations?

Quang the dwarf has stood there, Hang's 299 hopefuls have stood there, the man with jet-black hair and bicycle pump has stood there each evening and, most unexpectedly, brother Hung also.

One night, missing her twin sister's breasts, little Hoai could not sleep. She went to the window and could not believe her eyes: the computer engineer, red-hot graduate of Lomonosov University, pride and joy of the family, was locked in a passionate embrace with the mixed-blood dancing girl, the wager in that card game. They were drowned in a deep long kiss. Around them, the world switched off, the trees closed their eyes and feigned sleep, the wind tiptoed on the canopies, the stars drew a curtain to curb the light, the insects turned down their volume, and even the unfeeling naked light at the factory's security hut dimmed, leaving the lovers to themselves, intoxicated by the language of love as their bodies ripened in the fires of the flesh. They clung to each other, arms, lips and clothes intertwined, untangled then tangled again, like a cubist painting firmly fixed on the wall; and the wall shivered and trembled, sweated and trembled again, became blurred and gently melted into the tactful curtain of the night.

Three years later, Hung married a woman of twenty-six with an Asiatic nose; a university lecturer in Russian, intelligent, reasonable, of revolutionary background, who travelled to Russia for two months a year on placement, good at 'feminine' home duties: both husband and wife led an ideal life. But my brother could never purge from his memory the crazy and disastrous three-week love affair with that mixed-blood girl whom he now cursed. Poor brother Hung.

Teacher Hoang had mortgaged that girl to this medieval country and her new owner. She was in fact not difficult to please. She had only two needs: entertainment and spending money – entertainment without money was not possible; having money and not indulging herself was equally impossible – that was all. Her serial owners came and went, that did not matter, money came and went, entertainment fashions also came and went, they also did not matter. She remained. She did not support herself, she allowed others to look after her. She never thought about anyone or anything for longer than five minutes. She possessed a kind of exotic beauty that was possibly quite common in the bustling streets of Saigon, where it might be regarded as attractive but not stunning, but in somewhat staid Hanoi it caused a sensation. Her beauty was sensitive to time yet her nineteen-year-old soul was impervious to its passage, static and stagnant, the product of a lifelong dedication to skimming the surface, trusting herself to whims. She was wasteful and revelled in being narcissistic, blatantly flouting her unlimited capacity for vanity. Beautiful, liberal, innocent and unpretentious, she was almost a *Camille*, except for the substance.

She accepted Hac as her new owner without a word of complaint. She was there when he left home, she stood by as he ate; even when he closed his eyes, he would still feel her presence. Wherever he went she would faithfully follow. At kerbside tea stalls, when he sat down to smoke his pipe, she would sit next to him. When he stood up to leave, she would do the same. When he went home, she would follow close to his heels, with her deep blue eyes and ivory skin.

After several days he became irritated: 'What kind of woman are you, always clinging to my heels?' He wasn't used to this kind of attachment. He tried avoiding her but it didn't work. Neither did keeping a cold distance. Finally he told her to stay away. Afterwards, ironically, fate dictated that he fell in love with someone else who conspicuously lacked a sense of vanity, and he paid a huge price for that.

It was a wintry day in 1984, the coldest day that Hanoi had ever experienced. Hung was returning from a party where young men and women who had saved a bit of money from their frugal days as students overseas had gathered. They had also gleaned a little knowledge of the world and of foreign languages from those days, and a little experience of European culture – which was now invading this proud South-east Asian country, and was accepted without criticism as a progressive new trend, an inevitable imported revolution. They had nothing more interesting to do than go to parties, where they could rehearse their style and parade themselves, before sliding into self-repeating and endless office timetables. Returning from such a party, his footsteps echoing on the cold pavement, Hung was stunned to see a girl sitting by herself under the street lamp, head bent, looking utterly lost in her flimsy clothes, her lips a purplish blue from the terrible end-of-year cold.

Their short love story began with the young intellectual's pity for an unfortunate caught in the cruel twists of life. His initial, impulsive protective gesture (what would have happened if there hadn't been any red wine that night, if the pavement hadn't been so cold, the street light so bright, accentuating the cold lips?) was engendered first by noble instincts and feelings, and then grew so strong that it finally overwhelmed him, dictating his actions and persuading him to believe in his own behaviour. She was the victim of a despicable society, of imperialism and neocolonialism, of a slave culture and its crime. She was unfortunate, not guilty; she was without support and needing salvation. And it was he, he who came.

He extended his chivalrous arms. The dancing girl recognised the younger brother of her owner and did not decline. They talked; her lips remained purple. They went to the railway station for a meal; her lips remained purple. They went for a walk in the empty streets; her lips grew even darker. Finally he kissed her as if trying to bring a brighter colour to her attractive heart-shaped lips.

Despite five years in another country, several quick brushes with blonde-haired girls on dance floors and on the metro at rush hour, several passionless love affairs with fellow Vietnamese students, with no significant pain and misery, he had remained absolutely neutral and moderate in all aspects of life, a person whose success was essentially due to moderation, and to whom moderation equalled quality of life. But this once, and alas only once in his life, he lost himself in passion for a girl who possessed neither education, restraint nor etiquette. Like a finely bred and highly trained horse suddenly released for the first time, he succumbed to the intoxication of a beautiful wild flower and threatened to snap his tether. He had never come across anyone so vain yet so attractive. After the second kiss he had already mapped out the superficial nature, poor intellect and under-used brain of the beautiful girl in his arms. Marshalling all his reasoning skills to her defence, he still could not completely suppress a feeling of revulsion, the feeling of a clean-living person who had to put his hands inside a festering rubbish bin. But her face shone bright, expectant, grateful, admiring, her lips quivered, her eyes were so deep blue, her skin so milky white, her thighs so infinitely long and her gossamer-soft breasts pressed so close, that he felt insanely wonderful. She gave herself innocently, happy like a child receiving a present; she displayed her love-making skills as a skilful artisan his craft; she aroused and coordinated pleasure as he would his computer programs; she was unaffected by his inner turmoil, his balance between disgust and pleasure, between resolutely resisting yet happily surrendering himself to fierce passion.

Every night they pinned themselves against the wall under my window, acting out their love game, drenched in pleasure, oblivious of social custom, the law, their future, or public opinion. And the price they paid was the accumulated revenge of those rejected forces.

Of course my parents screamed abuse from morning to midnight, as the granite-paved future of their son, pride and joy of the family, risked collapse because of 'A slut who is only interested in your money!' Even Hac attacked him 'Why tangle with her? *I* couldn't get rid of her quick enough!' How his tone had changed since he had become the boss.

Predictably, such initial minor difficulties only served to enhance the intensity of their love, bonding them more closely. Each night the wall under my window trembled with more intensity. Love was more than love, it now had an added dimension of challenge and self-assertion.

The dancer would have gone on as long as there was enough money and amusement. So would Hung, if his immense sense of moderation hadn't prevailed. Their obstinate love affair might have continued a little longer had it not been for Hung's impending appointment.

Receiving a notification from the Ministry of Tertiary Education, he rushed to that famous address in Hai Ba Trung Street, his heart pounding: he had been waiting for nearly six months. The official who received him was quite cold and frank.

'Based on all assessment criteria and an acceptance from the authorities of another country, you qualify to be recommended for overseas study for a Master of Arts by research. Regrettably, however, according to our files, since you returned home you have been sustaining a close relationship with a person of dubious background and questionable means of support. She also has had a close relationship with another person, a traitor to the nation, who attempted to flee the country but was arrested and put into jail. We need to rethink your case.'

Sweat dripped down and soaked his back, and he developed a fever on the way home. That night the world again switched off, the trees closed their eyes and feigned sleep, the wind tiptoed on the canopies, the stars drew a curtain to curb the light, the insects turned down their volume, and even the unfeeling naked light at the factory's security hut dimmed; but my brother lay delirious, blaming himself, cursing life and the fateful love affair. When his health recovered, he tried to bury the three crazy weeks by waiting all day, every day at that famous address, mobilising all his assets – both material and intellectual – accumulated from his student days into making contacts and grovelling at appropriate doors, hoping to find a suitable girl-friend for a public and proper relationship. He didn't fail. He who persevered so much with such faith couldn't fail. Although unable to reclaim the admission ticket to the serious world of scholars, and although the bitter aftertaste was to be with him for the rest of his life, he accepted – for the time being – an official post at the Centre for Computing Research.

The address book didn't let him down. The Russian lecturer girlfriend proved to be the most suitable for his pressing plan for love and marriage. Within a short time the three disas-trous weeks with the exotic girl became just a toothache of his soul, short and sharp, but even-tually blunted by life's more pressing plots and plans. That was truly a time for self-affirmation. He returned to himself – a man of moderation who knew a little bit of everything, who was a touch passionate about everything, comprehensive but superficial, intelligent enough to be happy about himself, sufficiently kind to avoid causing others harm – the ultimate model and aspiration for the middle class.

Fate did not offer him dangerous twists or brilliant glory: things beyond the limits of mere mortals. Instead, he got married, bought an apartment, and one by one confronted the basic human concerns: oil stoves, salary rises, pilot projects, adding a mezzanine attic, children, learning a second foreign language, promotion, a fridge, the qualifying examination for research studentships, drinking beer with friends on Sundays. There would have been nothing worth talking about if the old toothache didn't simmer beneath, countering the pleasant taste of the middle-class banquet that he worked so hard for. The toothache was the only catastrophe in a life otherwise absolutely free of drama. Once, but alas only once in his life, having gone to the very end of the road of pleasure, having lost himself, experienced the utmost ecstasy and felt the tidal force of his own passion, he turned and ran away from it all, running from the destruction that lurks within all pleasure; in short, my brother chose to become an unfortunate man. But memory works like a piece of blotting paper. The program for love and marriage, life and success, runs through his computer-like brain, smoothly, without a glitch, input and output both perfect. He has neglected only one thing: memory, a critical factor.

My brother was not happy. For the rest of his life he was defensive, fearful of losing control once more, of losing his safe anchorage, his sense of moderation. Yet more than anything, he craved to lose himself, he missed that feeling of being engulfed by immense pleasures, feeling himself melting against the wall, dissolving into the unoccupied world of the night, hearing only the primal sounds of his body demanding love, love to the point of satiation.

The dancer wasn't sad for long. She soon discovered that the charming and chivalrous Lomonosov graduate was just a bland and boring engineer, punctual and dependent on his salary. She quickly found other owners. Sometimes she would be seen hand in hand with the man without a face, sometimes with a professor, white haired but still lovable; her fortunes rose and fell but she remained as vain and attractive as ever.

Another model somewhere between A and Z.

CHAPTER 17
The Woman Citizen

The verbal agreement to hand over the ice network of tropical Saigon took effect instantly as though it had been sent by telegram. Written contracts and official seals are not part of the underworld, where even paper-hungry officialdom fails to penetrate, and where life or death hang on a nod or a shake of the head, or sometimes even on a non-committal 'Uh-huh'. Less than fifteen minutes after that fateful game of cards, Bearded Hac was unanimously and politely acknowledged as the new ice-king by everyone whose livelihood depended on Saigon's ice network, from ice-delivery boys, transport men rushing smoking ice-blocks through the streets, confident café owners, suspicious smooth-talking characters, to the respectable officials who ruled the water and electricity supply systems.

The usurper of the throne was stunned by the perfect kingdom left by the deposed. His own numbers-game racket, thought to be so sophisticated, with a fine network of tentacles reaching into every hideout of Hanoi's leisurely citizens, with thousands of mobile sales representatives, with hundreds of stations operating at street level, all of a sudden seemed puny compared to the ice network. Even the busiest time for Hanoi's numbers game – between five and six o'clock in the evening – the hour when millions of hearts mortgaged to this semi-public gambling institution collectively skip a beat, seemed just a quiet holiday compared to the five a.m. starting hour of Saigon's thirst-quenching network.

Hac was stunned and impressed. This was Saigon, innocent yet humming with life, all-embracing but also pitiless, not knowing the meaning of forgiveness, following the only rules of existence: people always have to eat, indulge, make love and fully enjoy the regular afternoon rains.

Ten years before, Hac had cracked my parents' safe and stolen 300-odd piastres – their life savings – had taken the train to the south and lost all his money at restaurants, at untidy kerbsides, in salubrious avenues and on park benches. In the process he also lost the prickly pride and virginity of a young Hanoi man who had turned his back on education from the age of thirteen and who regarded himself as worldly. After he had spent his last cent, begged his last bowl of rice, slept his last night in a corner of the market among prostitutes, old women and petty criminals, the wayward son returned to Hanoi by train, this time not paying for a ticket as a matter of principle. His hair had grown to shoulder length, his beard was dirty and unkempt, his clothes were gaudy: he bore all the hallmarks of an important revolution, the transformation of a generation.

Returning to Saigon this time, my brother could look back at his earlier experience with a wry smile. Despite the change of ownership the ice network continued to operate efficiently. He spent six months studying the intimate workings of this beast, its rules of competition, the effects of advertisements, the advantage of a monopoly. He developed an admiration for its workings, silently wished teacher Hoang luck – his worthy predecessor's current whereabouts unknown – and then returned to Hanoi with three hundred taels of gold and a bold plan to reform the under-developed numbers-game network in Hanoi into a business like its southern cousin. My brother did not finish Year Seven but he was quite bright; he understood the need to modernise.

In the years to come, social historians will recall the 'numbers-game phenomenon' in the years 1986–87 in Hanoi. Together with *Mexico 86* and the television series *The Octopus*, 'numbers-game fever' became the hottest and most talked about topic of conversation. The whole population gambled. My brother can proudly claim dozens of innovations to the game based on permutations of numbers between zero and ninety-nine, elusively changing like a Rubik cube. Betting on the result of the state-run lotto, gamblers could choose any combination, first digit even and last digit odd, they could skip or follow a particular combination, they could bet on any 'patch' or 'field' of numbers, they could vary their bets to follow any mathematical progression, they could bet on numbers from the two extreme digits inwards and from the middle digits outwards, they could select their odds for a fixed payout, from 30 per cent to 300 per cent. Hac's innovations kept the regulars at their habit, induced the clean-living to have a little flutter for a bit of excitement, prepared a 'clearway' for those who had just had a big win, and egged on infatuated beginners to bet big.

Simultaneously the two networks, one south and one north, spat out huge profits. My world of four hundred brown glazed squares and an ever-changing magic window creaked under the weight of wealth – gold, jewellery and expensive furniture – and the weight of souls mortgaged to games of chance, and of lives hanging on an elusive 1 per cent. The pitiful bookcase had long been turned around; it now faced the wall. Father's trusty water pipe was neglected in a corner; he now smoked nice imported filter cigarettes. Mother had forgotten the terrible curses uttered on the day of little Hon's death. The rickety chairs were thrown into the kitchen to be used as firewood for cooking our now sumptuous meals. And the roof ceased to sing its briny teary songs.

When the termite-eaten food cabinet, despite its hearty protection by Che Guevara, had to go into the kitchen to make way for a new piece of furniture (a masterpiece of carpentry with dozens of drawers, engraved with traditional upper-class motifs of dragon, unicorn, tortoise and phoenix) mother cried because she couldn't believe that happiness was within her reach, and father's voice pensively dropped a pitch.

'In all my life I've never dared dream of something as fine as this.'

Hac shrugged. 'This is nothing, we must buy a house that is worthy of our talents and virtues.'

And little Hoai just held on tight to her window ledge, saying a silent good-bye to the rickety gate of the brewery with its constant yeasty smell.

But my family's story didn't end with a move to a house commensurate with our talents and virtues. Even long after tragedy had struck, my family still failed to understand what had hit them. It all started on the day of my sister's wedding, and she was the only one who suffered no consequences whatsoever.

The widow of the lottery agent was quicker than anyone else to understand the power of the boss of the underworld. She docilely placed herself and her children at his feet and turned the state lottery agency into an outlet for the numbers-game for a meagre commission. It seemed that her life was settled. It seemed that her undernourished insignificant self dared not occupy any other place. Nobody suspected that she harboured vengeance. On one pay-day, she introduced my brother to her best friend, a demure girl with long hair and fine skin, 'a decent woman, might even be a teacher'. And that demure beauty besotted my brother from the minute he saw her.

My brother trembled for the first time, after a life of casual contact with women of all kinds – upper-class women seeking forbidden thrills, *nouveau riche* women determined to have a good time, modern young girls seeking danger and excitement, and numerous girls of the night. He became a slave of that self-respecting girl, glowing happily for weeks at her smile and suffering for days from a frown on her smooth, flat face. Yes, deep down in his heart he had secretly dreamed of having a traditional, feminine wife, good children and a respectable family.

Six months later, after the lottery widow's energetic efforts as go-between, my brother scored his first success: she accepted his invitation to a movie; not *Ruslan and Ljudmila*, but a film shown at the same cinema which several years before had witnessed the absurd declarations of love by teacher Hoang for my twin sister. He sat paralysed in his seat, his plump proprietor body wedged tight between the arm-rests, and sweat trickled from the eight fleshy folds of the web between his fingers and the eight between his toes, despite the newly installed air-conditioning. He watched but did not follow the actions on the screen. Next to him sat the prim and proper girl, calmly watching the film of a habitual criminal finding salvation in love and changing his ways.

Time passes, yet fairy tales continue to beguile people.

At the end, the girl remarked, 'A wonderfully meaningful film.' And as if to reward him for taking her to such a good film, she agreed to go for a short walk along the best-lit section of the lake-side. Those fateful fifteen minutes were enough for her to enquire into his past, his thirty drifting years, and all the intimate workings of his business. Shyly she allowed my brother to put a huge ring on her dainty little finger and touchingly she advised him to find a more honest way to make a living. Still entranced, he could only manage to keep up a string of banal small talk, repeating her name as if fearful that it would be blown away in the lake-side breeze.

'So your name is Trâm?'

'Yes.'

'Yes, Trâm, mm ... You are a teacher?'

'No.'

'A child-care worker?'

'No.'

'Well, I give up ...'

'I am a citizen.'

When he got home, Hac picked me up, playfully threw me towards the ceiling and declared proudly, 'Do you know what it means to be a citizen? A citizen. You understand?'

I didn't know. I've never known. I've never

been regarded as a citizen. Only Quang the dwarf, who kept a complete record of everyone in the sub-district, knew what had happened to my rights as a citizen. But he hadn't spoken to me since my refusal of his marriage proposal.

Overwhelmed by his emotions and by this strange new language, my brother did not recognise the first ominous signs. The numbers-game network was modernised on the model of a successful Saigon business. But my brother forgot that, unlike the ice network, this was a gambling business where the potential to win or lose was roughly equal. He copied teacher Hoang but forgot to add his own signature. Later on when they faced each other again, behind bars, teacher Hoang laughed at the gullible young man.

Bad luck came in the middle of 1987 as my family was preparing to move to an elegant double-storey villa. For two weeks the state lottery, whose results determined the payout from my brother's illegal gambling racket, treated hungry gamblers with numbers ending with an odd digit. Gamblers celebrated. Hac stoically paid out seventy times their wagers. Day after day the same thing happened. The army of those chasing odd numbers swelled. The gold, precious stones and fine furniture accumulated in our home began to walk out.

What God gives God takes.

It was another terrible summer solstice day with a blue sky. People came to remove the dream of my parents' life, the masterpiece of carpentry with dozens of drawers, engraved

with dragon, unicorn, tortoise and phoenix.
Mother threw herself on the ground, the mouldy
water pipe rolled with her and father rolled after
it. The creditors, all of them without faces,
contemptuously glanced at the dilapidated four
hundred glazed brown squares, the pile of cheap
pots and pans, and the pale little girl standing at
the window. Hac sat there, playing with his
fingernails, looking piercingly at a fixed point on
the ceiling, deep in thought, considering
whether he should mobilise Saigon's ice to save
Hanoi's crippled gambling network or let go of
everything, start afresh a clean life and ask for
the hand of the woman citizen.

At that moment Quang the dwarf walked in
with steps far too long for his body, behind him
the cold professional face of the second lieu-
tenant of the local police, and ended my
brother's belated calculations.

'Come with me. Come and gamble with the
god of death.' Quang the dwarf never forgets,
never forgets an unpaid debt.

The figure-eight handcuffs glinted steely cold
in the 41-degree heat of the summer solstice.
Crowds of people converged as at all celebrations or executions. Father regained the confident posture of a cadre. 'Take him wherever you
wish. I disown him, I disown him.' Hac sleep-
walked away, muttering to himself, 'Odd, even,
even, odd.' Trâm, the girl with long hair and fine
skin, in her police uniform showing the rank of a
full lieutenant, took him to prison with the
encouragement, 'When your time's up, I will try
to find you an honest way to make a living.' She

had given the ring with the huge stone to the authorities, it being the crucial evidence forcing Hac to plead guilty to the crime of 'attempting to bribe an officer in the course of duty'. Thus she discharged her duties as a citizen.

Outside, without its head, the gambling empire disintegrated under effective measures by the authorities. On the other hand, the ice empire in Saigon continued to thrive. The lottery widow was given a reward large enough for her to start a kerbside stall serving tea, and selling lollies and cigarettes.

Each month, little Hoai would visit her unfortunate brother, taking a basket of supplies. He refused to see anyone else in the family and he chanted over and over the same mantra, 'Odd, even, even, odd.'

CHAPTER 18
Hang's Diary

19th

I have chosen you, a sister younger by less than a minute but so different to me, because I couldn't face confessing my sins to myself. The relationship between me and this 'self' has long been in a serious crisis. And between you and me there has always been a strong tie, mysterious but unchanged, constantly defying all odds. You're like a mute witness, intelligent, firm and decisive, and you've never turned your back on me throughout my crazy, compromised life. Right now I want to end once and for all this mad game by an equally mad action. I mean the balance has decisively tipped to one side. I mean there still exists a balance. I mean there still exist ties that bind. But, oh dear, I've begun to make things complicated ...

Where should I begin? Perhaps I'll start from this, this roll of toilet paper on which I'm writing. Not that I'm trying to be eccentric, I'm simply prone to impulses. I'm not sure when the idea of writing to you on this roll first occurred to me; I only know that before I was aware of it I had already started writing.

He, my respectable husband, has a very unusual preoccupation with toilet paper. In the middle of hundreds of things to do, amongst urgent preparations for an impending trip to Bonn – having just returned from Singapore he is about to jump across to West Europe, a superb athlete, don't you think? – with new developments of a *coup d'état* in Latin America to be assessed, with state receptions and national celebrations to be organised, he never forgets one thing: to replenish his stock of toilet paper. The reserve must be at least ten rolls, his minimum consumption for six months. If it ever falls below that level he becomes like a man sitting on a fire, he can't stay still as if bursting to go to the toilet, and can't concentrate on any serious matter. But then again, is there anything he does that I would regard as serious? At first I was amazed, I couldn't understand how those common rolls of paper, used only to serve an inelegant bodily function, could be of such importance to him. But after a while I began to understand. Married life does that to you, it offers us unique insights into each other and we end up seeing through each other's minds.

He is terribly attached to toilet paper. All his life he has been attached only to things that can be evaluated. Toilet paper is one of those that he values highly. For a very long time, he – you and I as well, a whole generation – never knew that there existed such a kind of paper reserved for a need that we went about without much fuss. And then for a long time we learnt that it was a luxury item, an immoral product of an ideology based on parasitic consumerism, not to mention its inhuman nature, given that there was not enough paper for children's schoolwork. For a very long time we steeled ourselves in our stoic mould, ignoring what we regarded as 'small matters' because there were important things in life more worthy of our attention. We advocated the importance of self-denial, attaching to it such virtues as simplicity, sacrifice and strength. This continued for a long time and became fashionable for a whole generation.

But then one day he went on official business to another society – was it Singapore? – and his whole set of values were shaken and shattered. I don't know what happened. I only know that in the new system of values that he brought home, toilet paper occupied a prominent place. It became an central part of his notion of human civilisation and dignity. It became so important to him that he now wouldn't know how to go about his natural business without it. A huge tragedy. Just as he wouldn't know his own character without expensive suits and soft leather shoes. But suits and shoes could be imported from Singapore or Bonn, and nobody could go through ten suits or a dozen pairs of shoes in six months. So in this regard he could rest assured, his character had enough in reserve to hold on until the next official trip. But toilet paper goes at an alarming rate: ten rolls every six months, impossible to replenish unless you are prepared to pay with foreign currency. In order to remain civilised and dignified in this manner, one had to be at least the wife of a corrupt minister or a rich businessman. But he was only a promising middle-ranking diplomat. So when those rolls of paper began to appear timidly in Hanoi, a mini revolution (they were of low quality but nonetheless different from the usual newspapers and student exercise books), he bought the lot, hoarded them, constantly fearful that this new-born consumer revolution might prove to be short-lived; after all, nothing lasts for long in this country of ours! Thus he became a hoarder of toilet paper.

Please forgive me for beginning this diary with a topic not all that romantic. But I know you are violently allergic to any notion of romanticism. It's the fault of the all-blurring fog of emotion that people throw in others' eyes. You are sceptical of emotional ties because you are too sensitive. You reject romanticism because you are the most enchantingly romantic person in the world.

If only I knew how to be firm like you.

I hope this story about these ugly toilet paper rolls will help fuel your anger at the pretensions that humans flaunt in the face of the fellow members of their species. This afternoon, returning to his home, assembled from so many shining philistine values, a silky cocoon of well-fed silkworms, he will go white in the face when he discovers that a whole roll is missing from his treasure. If I hadn't decided to send it to you I would have returned this roll to its proper place in the treasure house. And then one day, six months from now at the latest, in an unhurried and smug manner, he would open it and read a complete diagnosis of his sick obsession with toilet paper. There are so many other obsessions as well.

21st
If only beauty could be traded for something else. But what? I don't know what I want. I am both sceptical and envious of those who seem to know what they want.

I don't know when I became convinced that an unusual destiny awaited me. A glorious destiny, over and above the limit prescribed by the majority for the majority. The notion about this boundary is quite vague, it's more like a feeling. If I was prepared to go through to the end, to dig up this feeling, to stretch it out as one would the skin of a drum to its highest tonal pitch, if I could do that, perhaps I might be able to discover something more than simply a feeling; a feeling might then become an actual lived experience. But this is beyond me. Always emerging is the feeling of energy drain, of running out of breath, of weakening, of being born prematurely. I have never known how to pursue anything to the very end. Before I could learn to live life to the full I had succumbed to the habit of accepting comfortable but incomplete pleasures. Everything is half-baked. No red hot passion nor even blind hatred for me. I have started many things just to abandon them with a smooth shrug of the shoulders. Sketched so many ideas and plans but never followed them through. Incomplete, just like modern lifestyles. Just look at our modern painters, what have they been able to perfect? At best, they have managed to raise the level of incompleteness. Anyway, it's a kind of improvement.

So you see, I don't have the strength to live life to the full. Since I don't even know what I want, the only axis on which I can turn is my ego, my self; there is nothing apart from this self and its bland and girlish needs.

I am sceptical of other lives turning around other axes, and at the same time I envy them. At least they find happiness because they are so overwhelmed by outside pressures that they lose themselves, become so dependent that dependency becomes a matter of course and questioning it becomes meaningless. Perhaps those who seek freedom are the truly strong people, as freedom means being cut off from all safety, trusting oneself to oneself and being prepared to accept all eventualities. It is nothing but fear that causes most people to put a safety collar around their neck and become used to being governed by external pressures. Completely governed. There isn't enough space to worry about themselves.

They cannot and are not allowed to run out of steam. They are sucked up by the force of their fear, and it is not uncommon for them to achieve great feats.

As to our generation, what great feats await us?

Two great wars have passed and the medals now shine only during ceremonies. The great feats of the past have now been catalogued away in libraries where we can view them from a distance and in perspective. As doubt and boredom set in, our appetite for achieving heroic deeds has diminished and in this vacuum we now turn to half-baked entertainment instead. Money now holds the key to success and around me everybody dances around the money axis. The strong can defy its centrifugal force and stay with the money, the weak are thrown off as dictated by the law of natural selection.

As for me, my only focus is myself, nothing but my own self with its needs, basic but vain. And the feeling of running out of breath, of unfinished-ness – the essential feeling of my generation – continues to nag at me, while the desire for perfection won't let go. If only I could exchange beauty for something else.

For a bit of your determined silence?

23rd
He is making coffee, diligent as a butler, captivated like a bonze catching his head monk furtively eating dog meat. He said, 'You know, family happiness depends a great deal on the wife's skills in making coffee.'

I badly wanted to tip the tray over, right there and then, to watch the rippling brown liquid splash onto the rug underneath. Yes, mother never made coffee. Cold boiled water ruled supreme for all seasons. No wonder our family was not happy. But in the end the tray stayed where it was; only the inkwell was tipped over and ink splashed the tablecloth. 'Oh my God! It took me a lot of time and effort to find such an ideal tablecloth!'

He spent the whole evening rescuing the tablecloth and I, my self-pity.

26th

On our wedding night he lit candles. If it had been incense perhaps I might not have minded the smell of a strange man.

I took off my clothes automatically; as you know I hate those who would peel me off layer by layer like an onion. I took off my clothes one by one, unhurried and challenging, as I had done so many other times in my life. I stood in front of the mirror so that from behind he could admire the double images of my breasts. I thought of your soft, gentle, caressing hands. Only you are gentle and loving. Men only like to maul them in their own ways. In ten years they will have become such a misshapen mass that there will be no more mauling nor soft gentle caresses.

I sat down on the bed draped in pure white sheets, put on a well-rehearsed expression and closed my eyes, come what may. With eyes closed, all men are the same, don't you think?

They carry on with their business, I don't participate. Convenience. I only need them to leave
me alone so I can follow my own inert uncoop-
erative body wandering into a vast emptiness,
wanting to fall into a state of weightlessness yet
unable to, because waiting at the bottom of the
crevasse is the monster of the memory of a
seventeen-year-old, because nobody has awak-
ened in me the ultimate trembling, because the
touch of flesh on flesh can only send vibrations
to my outer husk. I closed my eyes, avoiding
even the kisses on my lips, kisses that would
leave an aftertaste stickier than making love to
oneself.

He approached, closer and closer, ten
centimetres, five centimetres, and when there
was only one centimetre left he collapsed onto
the bed, hugged my feet and cried with happiness. So my mirror performance achieved the
desired result. He finished his business, and
drifted into the sleep of a satisfied groom till the
morning. As always, I was left to myself, trying
not to think of the cold, sticky feeling on my
stomach and dreaming of an immediate shower.

29th
He said, 'Your whole complicated past I regard
as having not existed. But from now on you must
understand our position in society.'

A position reserved for me, of once a week
yawning furtively in a velvet armchair when he
lectures on *coups d'états* somewhere in far away
Latin America, when his boss lectures on even
more terrible *coups d'états* happening in the

yellow building next to President Ho's mausoleum, when his wife displays chronic anger about the injustices dished out to her husband by his colleagues (wives always know their husband's colleagues so well) and when their friendly daughter shares the addresses and private telephone numbers of well-connected socialites that I have to remember as part of my rite of passage. In this position, my beauty is a medal, family happiness is a medal, his career is a medal. With so many medals oppressing from all directions, where can I escape to?

Escape to you through this roll of paper?

He asked, 'What do you do with yourself all day? Write in your diary? You are not happy enough?' Yes, when overwhelmed by happiness one wouldn't need to write a diary.

Escape to bland love affairs?

He said, 'Don't abuse your privileges. You should learn to be reasonable. In the end you are quite common, just a little different to everybody else because of your beauty. Period!' Full stop. Have I put a full stop to my crazy life with this golden marriage? What about my unusual destiny? Am I just as ordinary as the rest of them?

30th

Three hundred times I burnt Ph, warded off fate and avoided the unpredictable, too frightened to face poverty and isolation, too hesitant to let go. On one end of the scale, I had put Ph, who didn't worship me, didn't worship anybody, who promised nothing, no ties that bind, no insurance, he loved only me but loved freedom even more; and on the other end the rest of the world of men, who pray and beg, fight and swear, encircling and tying me down.

Making a choice is something you can't avoid. Others can make what they will of my actions. They can nod their head in approval or frown in distaste, I don't care. The only two people who matter to me – you and the poet – are the only two people who didn't say a word.

Yes, what can one say when the woman in me refused to share the quiet humiliating fate of being the last surviving dreamer of this century, refusing the last haven that is mystery and void, refusing to lose herself in order to escape from the feeling of being half-way to insane pleasures, and rejecting freedom in the shape of loneliness? What else can one say? Nobody decides for anybody, and often the most daring decisions are borne out of coincidences or from the force of circumstances. Bold decisions can be made as long as there is a return ticket in hand, as long as they are forced by circumstances, and then decisions are not really decisions ...

I'm again complicating things. I didn't really need this much paper to tell you one simple fact: the poet will always welcome me. I'm going back to him. All these ridiculous games will dissolve in the gentle smile of the dreamer prince ...

* * *

The unfinished diary was left in the toilet paper reserve. The husband threw it at Hoai, disgust written on his face: 'I don't want to read what isn't meant for me. Professional ethics.' And before he elegantly turned on his heel to leave, he said, 'She'll come back in a few days. She's no longer at the age for playing hide-and-seek, for mysterious disappearances.'

True enough, Hang came back within a week. Since then I haven't heard her complain about her husband's crazy affliction, nor of having to yawn once a week in a velvet armchair. Her unusual beauty blossomed and within a short time she became one of the most well-known personalities in Hanoi. She is twenty-nine, one minute older than me, never to become a mother, even of a golden child.

The poet was arrested in the middle of a poem about the sea. Again it was Quang the dwarf who took him away. The poet and the Moon Goddess never met each other again.

CHAPTER 19
Magellan Journey

It was behind bars where the three faced each other: the ice-king, the numbers-man and the poet. Their three-way conversation was overheard by the prison guard, which made it impossible for him to live the rest of his life in peace. He had to dig a hole and bury the secret that he overheard. The flute that grew from the hole played me the following trio.

Teacher Hoang: Hey there, minor poet, you can have my rotten prison food. Can you tell me whether this is a piece of vegetable or a twig of grass?

The poet: Thank you. It's a vegetable.

Teacher Hoang: Once you are in here you've got to leave your pride behind. You must eat when hungry. Drink when thirsty. That's zen. Oh, but you stupid artistic lot wouldn't know anything about religion or philosophy! What sort of a country is this where writers and poets are all ill-educated? As far as I'm concerned I've disowned the word a long time ago. Eat first. You see, I don't want for anything. During my time here I've even put on weight. Stomach is bulging a bit. Lack of exercise. But I have no intention of sharing this roast chicken with you. That boy over there can go on pretending to be deaf and dumb, I don't give a damn. You can go on looking at that patch of sunlight on the wall. Every day it's the same patch of sun, even in your dream you dream of the same patch of sun. Nauseating. Got to have a drink. As to you, third-rate poet, you are welcome to eat my prison meal. Don't throw it away, that would be wasteful. Enjoy your meal.

The poet: Thank you.

Teacher Hoang: The poor little boy! Want to have a drink with me? Bit odd drinking by myself.

Hac: Leave me alone.

Teacher Hoang: You'll have to wait for another twenty-one days before your little Red Riding Hood comes with her basket of supplies. She is truly deaf and dumb. You only pretend. Your family must be a real nut-house. Why do you torture yourselves like that? Do you want to go on a hunger strike or something? For whom would your death be? Without you the world would just gain a little bit more room. One less melancholy face. Don't you think this prison cell is gloomy enough? Look at me ...

Hac: Keep quiet or I'll wring your bloody neck.

Teacher Hoang: Ah, so you want to be the bully. You want to establish your own hierarchy in here? What do you think, poet? You will stay out of this fight?

The poet: Yes.

Teacher Hoang: You see. My God, I can't figure it out whether it's me or the poor stupid little boy ...

Hac: Who are you calling a stupid little boy?

Teacher Hoang: Err ... I and the young stupid boy here have reasons to be here. At least we have had a fight. I wanted to get out of this bloody medieval country, he wanted to stay and become the uncrowned king of this backwater. In the end neither of us escaped – our meandering journeys converged at the same final point. The only difference is that I continue to feast on roast chicken and he spends his time fixing his nose to the patch of sunlight on the wall. And you, do you want to complete a revolution by poetry or what? Pity the minor poets – little and lightweight, yet holding so many illusions.

The poet: I don't share my journey with anyone.

Teacher Hoang: Ha ha. I've also had poems published under Hoang Van – 'Prince of Literature'. I've dreamt of becoming a Victor Hugo of this Annam. I've loved the most beautiful woman in this country; you also loved her, didn't you? Interesting games, but I am in here because I have finished with poetry, love and dreams, and you are here precisely because you have not. Twists of fate. Tell me, what crime did you commit?

The poet: I did not commit any crime.

Teacher Hoang: So they imprisoned an innocent?

The poet: That is their business.

Teacher Hoang: And your business is?

The poet: Poetry, love and dreams.

Teacher Hoang: I don't follow. Your poetry must have denigrated the regime or offended someone.

The poet: My poetry is only about my own life. I don't know what offending means.

Teacher Hoang: That sounds profound. Read out a poem for me. For a bit of fun. I am not quite an outsider, you know!

The poet: Mr Hoang, please return to your roast chicken and vodka. I don't write poetry to be read for a bit of fun. I am not concerned with the public, even though it may be the same public who reads the newspapers and magazines that published your poems, or a tactful armchair public. They can judge me in any way they like, they can worship or crucify me. Today I might be eating your scraps but tomorrow my place might be inside a gold-edged dictionary or atop a pedestal, which to me means the same thing. My journey is solitary, I don't need an audience, especially an audience the likes of you.

Teacher Hoang: It sounds good but let me tell you it's pure bullshit. I used to brag like that. You wait, life will teach you, your turn will come.

The poet: That is life's business.

Teacher Hoang: And my business is to laugh in the faces of those self-crowned saints and sages. In the end we're all the same. *La même chose!*

Hac: Enough, enough, my ears are burning. You talk rubbish.

Teacher Hoang: Hey, poet, you've found an accidental ally. Listen here, stupid boy, with your level of education, how dare you talk to intellectuals like that?

Hac: Shut up or I'll wring your neck back to front.

Teacher Hoang: How times have changed. Any little boy with a good fist can rule everyone else. That's how it is, my poet. After eight wandering years I've discovered that only two things can cow people: money and violence. Money can shut them up. Violence can also shut them up. In this medieval country the fist still rules. I understand. These stupid little boys have nothing other than their fists. What do they understand apart from the language of the fists? Let them be. But the beast of violence is so terrible. They resolve love affairs with razor blades, family quarrels with meat cleavers and business disputes with daggers. Few guns but many knives, and blood still has to be shed to the required volume. And any crass little dwarf can handcuff us. I understand, my little boy; one way or another you have to release the bottled-up energy within you. In other countries, people find release in harmless recreation such as art. Here the only opening for those like you is through violence. Once your mind has dulled, your muscles speak. You can wring my neck as much as you like but you will regret it. It will be me, nobody else, who will find you another escape, more civilised and not so brawny.

I don't like to resort to my fists, purely on aesthetic grounds, and also because I like to challenge myself. I like money much more; it's far more interesting and it has magic. There will be a time when money will domesticate the fist. Wouldn't that make life easier? Whatever you may say, I've devoted my life to building a shrine to money. The little boy sitting next to me proved to be a little inexperienced. The evolution from a medieval person to a modern man isn't necessarily the same as a change of ownership. It's no surprise that you failed, but you learned a major lesson. Very useful, because not you nor anyone like you or that bullshit saintly poet, none will escape the power of money. You'll get used to it, accept it and surrender to it unconditionally. You'll find true freedom with the permanent support of money, ha, ha, that is the essence of this era. This era acknowledges my work and that's why I am sitting here drinking vodka and eating roast chicken. And, my little boy who likes his fists, you'll live to see the day when your medieval knives and cleavers follow each other into museums. It won't be knives but guns that rule. I tried to escape to complete that final mission. The loss of one round is the beginning of another. Just as I told you: the world doesn't belong to poetry, love or barbaric fists. Like it or not, you are still in my palm, you must dance to my tune.

Hac: Fuck your mother.

The poet: You are the most ineloquent orator that I have ever met.

Teacher Hoang: I don't mind your abuse. It's quite common to resist first and surrender later. Young man, you will be released from jail and find a clean way of making a living, marry a good wife, have the regulation two children, and observe the responsibilities of a citizen. But it is your middle-class life that will propel you to me. It's the same with you, my poet. You must eat before you can write poetry. Even Buddha couldn't refuse a bowl of milk. I'll just sit here and wait for you to come and kneel down in front of me.

Hac: I'll wring your bloody neck!

The poet: Don't worry about him.

Teacher Hoang: Don't pretend, you have surrendered long ago. The scraps of food and the patches of sunlight will follow you through your life. Ha, ha ... Yes, there is also the matter of love. This young boy fell for a scab of a cop, and the poet's beauty is now happy in a golden cage, after her futile struggles. I am reassured that she is there. She also must dance to my tune. She leaves her saint to rot in jail. The saint who never tasted the fresh-honey taste of her flesh. And I, I took her when she was still adolescent, and I will take her again. Oh my God! Stop! Stop! Please, it hurts! Stop please ...

The prison guard intervened almost in time. Teacher Hoang gave a few moans before he collapsed unconscious, shards of the shattered vodka bottle piercing his skull. My brother and the poet, dangerous and violent elements, were immediately isolated. From then on the ice-king was no more.

Eight months later my brother was released and corrected my impression about the hand-cuffs. No, they didn't feel cold, even on the summer equinox. When they locked them on, my brother didn't know what he felt. He has now stopped chanting the old mantra about odd and even numbers. He now has a new habit: measuring the remainder of the day by the posi-tion of the patch of sunlight cast on the wall.

Twenty months later the poet returned: no conviction, no trial, not even a release order. It's only twenty months of a human's life.

CHAPTER 20
The End

THE TRANSFORMATION OF A
HOMOSAPIENS-A
OR A TRUE STORY ABOUT
AN UGLY DUCKLING

Every evening without fail, I watch the man standing outside the window and he follows with his eyes a girl with delicate shoulders, delicate to the point of melting into the yeasty scent from the brewery. Every chase is the same.

The man would stand there with his bicycle pump, paying no attention to complaints by clients – Homosapiens-A and Homosapiens-Z transformed by the rush hour – his eyes fixed on the two delicate shoulders until they became just two question marks lost in the chaos of the traffic. Then one day he left his pump, left my window and followed the two question marks.

The girl stayed silent. He remained quiet. Until the girl said, 'Please don't follow me like this. Tomorrow I am getting married.'

The man returned to his bicycle pump, and at the precise moment when he was about to turn to leave the brewery with its unspoken greetings, he suddenly noticed little Hoai at the window. He smiled and I smiled too.

'I've waited for you for fifteen years,' I said simply.

'Me also,' he replied calmly.

'Take me with you, please.' The man nodded and put his hand through the window, the first time I had touched a man's hand.

'Please wait for me to say goodbye to my parents.' I left the window. Less than five minutes later I was next to him, ready to leave the four hundred brown squares and the magic ever-changing window behind, taking with me only the twenty dried roses, Hang's diary and the remaining ashes from the three hundred Phs.

'Take me with you, please.'

The man stared at me in bewilderment and looked longingly at the space that little Hoai had just left.

'Excuse me, who are you? I'm sorry ... I'm meeting someone else, a little girl ...'

For fifteen years I waited, clinging onto the window ledge, contracting myself to the extent of losing my voice, and now at the decisive hour, I decided to become a 29-year-old woman, beautiful, the image of my sister Hang. My man has come, has smiled at me. I extended my two beautiful hands with their tapered fingers towards him.

'Take me with you, please.'

'I'm waiting for my little girl,' he said. He waited and waited in increasing hopelessness and then left, dissolving into the surrounding loneliness.

It was a day in early 1988.

Hanoi, February 1988

Afterword

The author's real name is Pham Thi Hoai Nam. Born in 1960 in Hai Duong province, she grew up in North Vietnam and in 1977 went to Germany to study at Humboldt University. She returned to Vietnam in 1983 to live in Hanoi where she worked as an archivist and began to write. Her translation into Vietnamese of Jorge Amado's *The Swallow and The Tom Cat* was published in 1986 and Frederic Durrenmatt's *The Judge and His Hangman* in 1987. Her first novel *Thien Su* (*The Crystal Messenger*) was published in 1988 and since then she has published essays, two collections of short stories *Me Lo* (1989), *Man Nuong* (1995) and another novel *Marie Sen* (1996). *Thien Su* (*The Crystal Messenger*) has been translated into French, Spanish, Italian, German, and Finnish. In 1993 Pham Thi Hoai left Vietnam for Berlin where she now lives with her partner and their child. In the same year the German translation of *The Crystal Messenger* was awarded the *LiBeraturpreis*, awarded each year at the Frankfurt Book Fair for the best writing by a woman writer from Asia, Africa or Latin America. In 1994 Pham Thi Hoai was awarded a City of Berlin literary grant in recognition of her writing.

In Vietnam her writing drew enthusiastic acclaim from readers and literary critics. Her detractors were just as vocal. Vietnam's cultural bureaucrats objected to her critical views of contemporary Vietnam, and were offended by her lack of respect for traditions and disregard of social taboos. For decades politics and literature in Vietnam have been interlinked and, as a result, the landscape of literature was dominated by a gaping fissure along ideological faultlines. With the ascendancy of the Marxist point of view, writers and artists were expected to participate in the national struggle, to serve the people and to support the common cause. Running more deeply is a more traditional view which regards literature as an instrument for the betterment of society. Pham Thi Hoai's writing is somewhat at odds with both of these expectations.

Despite having been attacked in a public forum, Pham Thi Hoai has never been accused of political dissent. Instead, her detractors have charged her with holding an 'excessively pessimistic view' of Vietnam, of abusing the 'sacred mission of a writer', and even of 'salacious' writing. But even her strongest critics acknowledge that she is a writer with a keen eye for detail, a humorous, acerbic wit, and a fine ear for the rhythms of the Vietnamese language.

Ton-That Quynh-Du